SAILOR'S DELIGHT

ROSE LERNER

SAILOR'S DELIGHT
Copyright ©2022 by Susan Roth

Cover by Kanaxa

This book is a work of fiction. The names, characters, places, and incidents are products of the writer's imagination or have been used fictitiously. Any resemblance to actual persons, living or dead, or actual events is entirely coincidental.

All rights reserved. This book or any portion thereof may not be reproduced in any form or by any electronic or mechanical means, including information storage and retrieval systems, without written permission from the author, except for the use of brief quotations in a book review.

RoseLerner.com

Table of Contents

Acknowledgments

I n part, this is a book about the trust between client and professional expert. Hopefully, I am not making it weird by thanking all the professional experts in my life, who have earned my trust (and frankly, my awe) again and again over the years. In particular: my cover artist, Kanaxa; my copyeditor, Kim Runciman; my formatter, Matt Youngmark; my sensitivity reader, Aleksei Valentín; my accountant, Charlene Fleming; and my agent, Courtney Miller-Callihan. I feel so lucky to have you all in my corner. Please know that I never take your talent or skills or generosity for granted.

On the flip side, I'd like to thank my own freelance clients. I'm humbled by your trust, and I've done my very best to repay it. Where I may have fallen short, I hope you can forgive me.

The first seeds of this story were planted in conversations with Olivia Waite, and she encouraged me to grow them. Elsa Lepecki Bean inspired me to make Elie my hero, and her portrayal of his family brought them vividly to life for me. Susanna Fraser and Tiffany Gerstmar gave kind, brilliant feedback; Gregory Holt and Tiffany Ruzicki did the same on multiple drafts, and our conversations opened up the story structure for me. Branen Salmon solved a key plot problem.

Thanks to the many Jewish and/or naval historians whose work helped me write this book, in particular Geoffrey Green,

Evan Wilson, Amy Miller, and Nicholas Blake. Allegra Rosenberg shared her research, and Shireen Bishop put me on the track of Guernsey frocks. My uncle David let me borrow his books and incidentally taught me most of what I know about sailing and the Royal Navy. Without all of you, this book would have been much poorer.

My esteemed Patreon patrons: I hope it isn't vulgar to acknowledge that *I* would have been much poorer without all of you! I thank you, most humbly, for your ongoing support, input, wisdom, and enthusiasm.

Jellybones Jones, I'll never admit this again so make the most of it: you are, in fact, the boss of me now.

For Uncle David

WHO KNOWS SUCH

USEFUL THINGS

I

Portsmouth, Hants.

FRIDAY, 24 SEPTEMBER 1813 / 29 ELUL 5573

Rosh Hashanah begins at sunset

Traditional wardroom toast:
"A willing foe and sea-room."

Eleazar Benezet looked at the mess on his desk with a sinking heart.

The box for incoming documents overflowed, papers stirring practically with each breath he took. A receipt drifted to the floor with a spiteful rustle. There were spikes on his desk for precisely this purpose. Was it asking too much that people use them?

The box for outgoing correspondence was empty. Everything to do, and nothing yet done. This wasn't how he'd planned to begin the new year.

It was no one's fault, Elie reminded himself firmly. His childhood friend Jael hadn't planned to begin the new year dealing with a house-fire, untimely widowhood, and baseless rumors that she'd murdered her husband, either.

…Probably the rumors were baseless. Probably she hadn't planned to.

Probably when he cleaned at Pesach, he'd find a stray bill behind a piece of furniture, now in arrears and accruing interest at twenty percent.

Still, he'd *agreed* to spend those three weeks in Rye Bay just before the Michaelmas quarter day, putting Jael's affairs in order. He'd known he would come back to paper drifting about his office like flakes of ash on the breeze. He was already wearing his oldest, ugliest, most comfortable clothes on purpose so he could crawl about peering under the furniture and getting dust up his nose. Whining about it was a waste of precious time. It was already seven a.m., and he had to be at the synagogue by sunset, which would be at…

He checked his luach, and remembered that he still hadn't bought a fresh one for 5574. This one stopped short today, its end-papers filled to the edge with jotted notes waiting to be copied over into next year's calendar.

Still, it told him that today's sunset would be at 5:57 p.m.—but that was in London. In Portsmouth (thank Heaven for small blessings!), the sun lingered an extra five minutes. He'd walk back to his aunt's house at five, to scrub off the dust and shave before the evening service.

He'd start by skimming and sorting all the papers he could see, in case something urgent was buried alive at the bottom of the box. Elie seemed to take on new responsibilities at Benezet & Sons every year, in addition to his perennial work for the firm as a navy agent, managing the affairs of absent sailors by power of attorney.

Elie was proud that so many people trusted him (not least his uncle Simeon, senior partner of Benezet & Sons). But on mornings like this, it also made him a little nervous.

He set the alarm on his watch for five. That was only ten hours of agonizing dullness. It could be worse.

No "I'll just scribble a quick reply, it'll only take five minutes," he reminded himself as he broke the seal on the first letter. It never *did* take five minutes, and—

Enclosed receipts cascaded onto his blotter.

Elie managed to shove them onto a spike without losing any, but his brief flare of triumph faded when he saw what they were: copying fees on the prize case for the *Vliegende Draeck,* a Dutch merchantman captured by HMS *Cocksure* in 1809 and tied up in the courts ever since.

"More like *Vliegende Drek,*" Elie muttered. Maybe it couldn't be worse.

He reset his watch alarm for four-thirty. There. He could manage nine and a half hours of agonizing dullness. Dull agony. Whichever.

You can take an hour for luncheon, he cajoled himself. *No dunking ship's biscuit in tea at your desk today.* He reset the alarm for noon. *There, only eight and a half hours of dull agony! Go on. Do your work.*

He sat in his chair, not doing his work.

This is your own fault, he told himself, much less kindly. *If you'd started the final* Vliegende Draeck *accounts as soon as the shipowners' last appeal was denied a month ago, maybe by now you'd only have four or five hours of agony left.*

He should never have taken the contract to prepare the accounts in the first place—only he knew Dutch and he was already familiar with the case, and he would have had to explain to Uncle Simeon *why* he wanted to snub Captain Willing's prize agent by turning down a simple bookkeeping job.

Setting his private reasons aside, a month's delay in completing final prize accounts was nothing. The ship and its contents had long since been broken up and sold, the money safe in the Bank of England. The first general distribution wouldn't be until the *Cocksure* returned home from foreign service in the spring, and none of its officers or men who'd since transferred to other postings were in port. Most were currently blockading Flushing on HMS *Steadfast*, commanded by Captain Willing's former first lieutenant.

Including Elie's favorite client, Augustus Brine, formerly sailing master of the *Cocksure* and now master of the *Steadfast*. Who incidentally planned to finally marry his childhood sweetheart when his prize money came in.

Prize money was distributed in extremely uneven fashion. One eighth went nearly whole to the captain, the next eighth was shared by the wardroom (the other commissioned officers, plus a few senior warrant officers like the master), and so on—ever smaller shares until the last eighth was divided up among all the common seamen, often hundreds of men. Augie Brine would receive twelve hundred pounds from the *Vliegende Draeck*. Hardly a fortune, but more than enough to set up a household.

Elie wasn't delaying on purpose…exactly. He'd been on the point of beginning when he'd been called away by Jael's disaster.

Probably on the point of beginning.

Not that being married would put Augie Brine any further out of Elie's reach than he already was. Really, it would be *better* if Brine were married. The final appeal, denied at last.

Maybe then Brine would spend his shore leave with his wife, instead of boarding with Elie's aunt and forgetting to close his door in the morning while he shaved without his shirt on.

Elie sighed and unlocked his secretary, retrieving the bundle of *Vliegende Draeck* papers from their pigeonhole and opening it on his desk. He unfolded the first document.

…Mr. Brine, my sailing-master, showed great coolness and decision…

…this brought us perilously near the shore, but Mr. Brine, having taken soundings in a boat the previous night, assured me that…

…a sudden squall from the S.S.W. was nearly our undoing, but Mr. Brine's prompt setting of the mizzen and fore staysail…

Elie gently refolded Captain Willing's log extracts and let his forehead *thunk* onto his folded arms. "Mr. Brine was exceedingly handsome throughout the whole of the engagement," he muttered. "The wind being southerly, his hair was blown about his face to great advantage. It is much to my men's credit that they did not permit this circumstance to distract them from their labors."

He would give himself one minute, and then he would begin. Sixty seconds…fifty-nine…fifty-eight…

Elie's watch alarm woke him at noon. He groaned. So much for taking an hour for his luncheon.

Cheer up, he told himself dryly. *Only five hours of agony left today.* But he looked at the box for outgoing correspondence, still bare as Old Mother Hubbard's larder—

Ugh, and of course there was a spider in it. He scooped it up in his handkerchief, and leaned out the window to shake it out.

"Hallo, Elie! Surrendering the counting-house to the French, are you?"

Elie stuffed his white handkerchief back in his pocket and made a rude gesture at his cousin Samuel. "There was a spider on my desk."

"Well, it's saved me climbing the stairs. Did you hear *Steadfast* anchored late last night? The Navy pay clerk went out this morning to pay them off. Our wherry's leaving from the Point in half an hour."

Elie started. "*What?*" He barely caught his hat before it fell into the street.

Samuel filled his barrel chest with air and cupped his hands to his mouth. "THE *STEADFAST* ANCHORED LAST NIGHT—"

"But the *Steadfast* is in the North Sea!"

"She was recalled a fortnight ago." Samuel peered up at him. "I left a note on your desk. A letter came from Augie Brine, too."

Elie cursed viciously and silently. "…I haven't quite finished sorting my correspondence."

"How could I forget what a busy and important man you are? Well, get your busy and important arse to the Point if you want to make the boat. We've got to be back by sunset."

Elie ducked back inside and, with impressive self-command, did not slam the window. Half an hour wasn't much time, but he pawed through the overflowing box for Brine's letter anyway. Papers sloshed over the side. There was no help for it; he'd have to look later.

Elie combed his hair, ran his tongue over his teeth, and shoved a memorandum book into his pocket with his used-up calendar. *Why* hadn't he bought a new one yet?

At least his pack was already well stocked with new shirts, stockings, blankets, buttons, needles and thread, pens and paper, pocketknives, precision watches, and so on, which Elie replaced from the Benezet & Sons warehouse downstairs as he sold them. Now he had only to slide in the requisite client ledgers, his coin purse, and copies of the new uniform regulations and *The Naval Chronicle*. Was there time to stop at the baker's before boarding the wherry? Clients were always in a better mood if you fed them.

Elie checked his watch. He could make it if he hurried. Putting on his overcoat and pack, he ran down the stairs—

—Only to race back up them a moment later to retrieve a heavy, distinctively curved box from the depths of the secretary, nestling it into his pack beneath a stack of beribboned straw hats.

Over the years, Elie had got used to climbing a ladder onto a rocking ship, but today it was nerve-wracking again. A Marine had shot a trader just a couple of weeks ago, because— well, it wasn't entirely clear why. Because his wherry hadn't been queuing properly, supposedly, although the Marine had also addressed the wherry's passengers as "Jew-looking buggers."

(Poor Mr. Veall, as far as Elie knew, was neither a Jew nor a bugger. Elie couldn't say the same for himself, which did nothing to soothe his nerves.)

Only navy agents like Elie could sell to sailors on credit, but anyone and everyone could sell to a sailor who'd just received several months' accumulated wages in cash. And since most of the men weren't allowed shore leave for fear they'd desert—especially in home ports—anyone and everyone brought their wares to the ship. A man-of-war on payday was an orgy, gin shop, gaming den, and open-air market rolled into one.

The orgy was more or less encouraged, but as the Navy already gave their men enough liquor to float another, smaller navy, they discouraged the gin; hence the need for queuing and inspection and the occasional bullet.

Mr. Veall was recovering, thank Heaven. But Mr. Abrahams hadn't, a few years before—the mildest-mannered fellow you could ever hope to meet, and the judge had only fined the Marine six shillings and eightpence for his murder.

Regulations were supposed to have been tightened, after that. Marine sentinels were supposed to only have blank cartridges, and their Armorers were *supposed* to inspect their cartouche boxes regularly to ensure it. And yet.

Still, no use thinking about what he couldn't see above the brim of his hat. At least the *Steadfast* was a frigate, with barely two decks above the waterline, and at the moment none of her sailors were humorously pelting him with anything. This too would pass.

Sure enough, just as he began to feel he'd be climbing forever, he tumbled onto the deck. "Open your pack," snapped the waiting Marine.

He'd known it was coming, but his heart stuttered anyway. He set the pack on the deck, but his fingers, stiff from the cold wherry ride, fumbled at the buckle. The impatient Marine jerked it away to open it himself, stretching the drawstring as wide as it could go.

"Easy!" Elie reached out. "There are—"

A second Marine leveled his bayonet.

Elie cringed back. "…delicate things in there," he finished under his breath.

The first Marine tipped the pack towards himself to peer inside. "Like rum bottles, you mean?"

"As you were, private," snapped a familiar voice with unfamiliar cold brutality.

The bayonet swung upright at once, and Elie wobbled. A supportive hand landed just below his shoulder blades. "Steady on," the voice said cheerfully. "You'll get your sea legs in a moment."

Elie's sea legs weren't the problem. Honestly, the bayonet might not be either.

"And go easy with my agent's pack, Mr. Polly," Brine rapped out.

"Sir!" The Marine came sharply to attention, releasing the pack—which promptly toppled over. Raspberries rolled across the deck.

Elie closed his eyes briefly. "Those were for you." Fat and fresh and perfect—or they had been when he'd bought them on impulse from the fruit-stand on the Point. He fished out the half-empty pottle and moved to kneel on the deck.

Brine's hand shifted to his arm, pulling him up. Gently, he pried the straw cone from Elie's cold fingers and handed it to the Marine. "Mr. Polly spilled them, and Mr. Polly will retrieve them."

The Marine obeyed, darting Elie a resentful look.

Elie's skin crawled. He ignored it, heaving his pack upright to check the rest of its contents. One or two straw hats would need mending, and the crown challah he'd bought to serve his other clients was dented, but the sturdy wooden box looked unscathed. The gift inside felt spoiled anyway. Nothing ever went how he imagined it.

But what had he imagined, anyway? What was the point in buying fine ripe raspberries for someone else's betrothed?

"Don't worry," Brine said. "I make very sure they follow

the regulations respecting blank cartridges."

Elie would prefer not to be hit with a blank cartridge, either.

The hand swung him around to face a well-worn blue and white uniform. "Won't you shake my hand, Mr. Eleazar? It's good to see you."

Elie took a deep breath. His lungs did their best, anyway. Wishing desperately that he'd put on a better suit this morning, he raised his head.

2

Between meetings, Elie tried to tell himself Augie Brine wasn't really that attractive. And then he saw him, and it was as if… Elie didn't know. As if he'd got used to wearing tinted spectacles, and then took them off and saw the full prismatic spectrum. *Oh, this is how colors are meant to look. I forgot.*

It wasn't mere physical beauty. Taken individually, Brine's features were good but not extraordinary: deep-set eyes, pale and piercing; broad cheekbones, one broken; full lips; engagingly crooked lower teeth that showed when he grinned, as he was doing now; tanned, weathered skin; a mop of light-brown curls, frizzing and unevenly bleached by salt and sun; broad shoulders and slim hips. His arse was arguably something out of the common way, but it was hidden by his coat-tails. (At least this particular outrage of naval discipline was softened by two gilt buttons just where the dimples above his buttocks must be.) And he was a trifle below average height, Elie admitted—reluctantly, Brine being precisely of a height with himself.

No, the secret was in the way he stood, the light in his eyes, some quality in his expression at once spiritual and puckish, as though a seraph were telling you a dirty joke. When he clasped Elie's hand, a subtle buzzing radiated from the point of contact to every nerve-end.

In short, if Augie Brine hadn't already had a better-paying job as a sailing master in the Royal Navy, he could have hired himself out to traveling lecturers as proof of the existence of animal magnetism.

The first Marine sentinel, plainly aware of Brine's eyes on him—presumably in rather a different way than Elie was—although surely at least a few crew members weren't immune… *Anyway,* the sentinel gave the pack a remarkably cursory inspection, and instead of dismissing Elie with a sharp jerk of his head, he said, "Passed, thank you, sir."

Brine drew Elie aside, out of the way of the next trader swarming up the ladder behind him. "How have you been?"

Elie shrugged. "Well enough."

"You'll make my cabin your floating counting-house, I hope."

Patches of red moved at the edges of Elie's field of vision: red coats, red berries. Mr. Polly chased down the last survivors, scarlet smears on the white deck all that remained of fallen comrades. Elie had wanted to give him something fresh and sweet, good luck for the new year, after Brine had been eating stale, boiled, pickled stores for who knew how long. Instead it was just more blood and gunpowder and brutality.

But Brine didn't seem to see any taint when the Marine at last presented the battered, dirty berries. He picked one off the top, blew away the dust, and popped it in his mouth, eyelids fluttering shut with a low moan.

Elie counted out four seconds in which he was permitted to simply look. Then he took out the wooden box. "This is for you, too."

Brine recognized its curved shape at once. "A new sextant!" But his face fell when he opened it.

"Is something wrong with it?" Elie thought he could appraise a sextant as well as anybody in Portsmouth, but—

Captain Hope, striding by, stopped short with a whistle. "A fine way to spend your share of the *Draeck* prize, Mr. Brine! May I have a look?"

Brine handed over the case. "You may have it altogether, sir, if you care to pay for it. You'd better find me a cheaper one, Mr. Eleazar."

Elie sighed in relief. "Is that all?"

Brine's eyes followed the gleaming instrument. "I can't spend the *Draeck* money. Once I've repaid what you've laid out for me over the last few years, the balance will be for my wife and mother-in-law to live on."

"Can we collect our shares yet, Mr. Eleazar?" Hope asked eagerly.

So much for Elie's relief. He knew the young captain well, having had charge of his finances before Hope had passed the lieutenant's exam and acquired a prize agent instead—a far more prestigious job than navy agent, handling larger accounts at twice the commission. Brine really should have hired one too after his own promotion to the wardroom, but he'd said he trusted Elie and would stick with him.

"I haven't completed the final accounts yet, sir," Elie admitted. "I've been away on urgent business the last few weeks, and… You know how the Ordnance Board is," he finished weakly.

Brine's woebegone face brightened with what must have been valiant effort. "Who doesn't?" He gave Elie a consolatory backslap that almost took his sea legs out from under him. "A friend of mine once received his ordnance money nearly six months after initial distribution."

"I've heard worse." Hope shook his head sagely. "Outrageous inefficiency."

They canvassed the outrageous inefficiency of the Ordnance Board for a couple of minutes before Elie said casually, "Of course if you don't want the sextant, Brine, I can easily find another buyer, but I paid only eighteen shillings for it."

Eyes widening, Brine made a swipe for the box.

Captain Hope held it out of his reach, laughing. "Oh, no, possession is nine-tenths of the law!"

Brine crossed his arms. "You're lucky we're in view of the crew and I'm obliged to show you the respect due a superior officer, *sir*."

"Yes, I trade shamelessly on my rank." Hope surrendered the box. "Alas, I can't afford even eighteen shillings after all the dinners I've poured down your insatiable gullet."

"Just for that, I'll eat all the raspberries myself." Brine ran a loving hand over the smooth wood. "You're the best agent in the business," he said with feeling.

Elie felt a pang of guilt. He *was* a good agent, but he didn't bring every client raspberries. And he'd paid a full guinea for that sextant—*before* he'd talked his cousin Morris (an optician) into grinding scratches out of the lenses and filters, and his cousin Gideon (a brass founder) into polishing the body. Elie had oiled the shabby case himself.

But Brine had been using the same sextant for nearly as long as Elie had known him. In point of fact, Elie'd discounted that one too, but neither of their pockets had stretched to much in those days, and now half the filters were cracked and the tangent-screw grew more temperamental by the week. And Brine was expected to pay for all his own equipment, even though he'd taken a cut in salary to transfer to a smaller ship with young Captain Hope, who'd been nervous to take his first command and who still struggled with the finer points of spherical trigonometry.

Every soul aboard relied on Mr. Brine to not run them onto a reef. It was practically Elie's patriotic duty to subsidize the *Steadfast*'s navigational equipment. And it wasn't as though *Elie* had a wife and mother-in-law to maintain, or ever expected to.

And Brine was already holding the sextant to his eye to take the sun's altitude. "Would you look at that?" he breathed happily. "Both limbs!" That meant the tinted filters had brought the sun's whole rim crisply into relief through the hazy clouds.

Brine locked the sextant in his trunk as soon as he'd led Elie into his cabin—not his sleeping cabin below, fortunately for Elie's powers of concentration, but the one on the upper deck for his charts and equipment, all stowed at present. The space was an unspeakable luxury at sea, but on land it might have done for a short scullery maid if you took out the eighteen-pounder.

Elie's eyes lingered on the cannon. *Who by water, and who by fire?* He desperately didn't want Augie Brine to die this year.

He said the blessing for bread under his breath as he drew the crown challah from his pack and unwrapped it. There hadn't been time to buy honey, but the round loaf was a wish for a round year, a full turn of the seasons; Elie would take a little bitterness over a sweet year cut short. Hopefully HaShem wouldn't dock him—or his clients—for the dents in the loaf.

And sailors were starved for fresh-baked bread. Brine, locking his trunk, straightened and spun on his heel at the smell.

Elie laughed and tore the loaf open. "Want some?" That got a broad, dazzling grin. It was another scientific mystery, how some smiles could be sweet enough to substitute for honey, yet so lethal you could have sold them wholesale to the Ordnance Board. Elie was suddenly aware that they were alone in a narrow, nominally private space, even if the partitions were movable and half window.

"Our new year begins tonight," he managed. "May you be written for a good year." Their hands brushed as he passed Brine a fistful of bread. Elie quashed the impulse to stick his fingertips in his mouth as though they'd been scalded.

"It's warm," Brine murmured huskily, and it took Elie a moment to realize he meant the challah. "Oh dear God," he said with his mouth full. "Fresh bread. Oh *God*." He shoved the last chunk in his mouth, slanting a brief, covetous glance at the loaf.

Elie almost handed over the whole thing.

"I'll post a Marine outside… A trustworthy one." Brine hesitated, licking a stray crumb from the corner of his mouth. "To guard my new sextant." And he was gone with a playful salute.

Elie drew his first deep breath since coming aboard, and set his ledgers on the table. Drat, he'd forgotten to ask Brine when he wanted to go over his own account. Did Brine think he already knew? If only he'd had time to find that letter!

The promised Marine took up his position outside the door. Truthfully, Elie would have felt more comfortable in the chaos of the lower deck, despite the apparent advantages of a secured, quiet cabin. But he couldn't expect Brine to see it that way. Marines protected him from his men every moment of all their lives. The Marines even slept between the officers' berths and the men's hammocks.

And Elie knew when Brine's solicitude had started. A few years ago, two drunk sailors had thought it very funny to dangle Elie by his heels over the *Cocksure*'s hold and shake him for loose change.

Mr. Brine hadn't thought it was funny.

Neither had Elie, obviously, but Brine's blazing, white-lipped rage had alarmed him. Was Brine a petty despot after all? The men had seemed equally shocked, however, so Elie had…

…Well, Elie had been flattered, and privately haggled Brine down from recommending flogging—which appalled Elie on principle, his vengeful impulse in this specific case notwithstanding—to a spell of hard labor at the pumps.

The whole thing, in short, had been a disgrace to all concerned, and Elie wished he weren't too thrilled by Brine's thoughtful gesture to reject it.

Still, the afternoon passed quickly enough in going over accounts, selling the contents of his pack, and engaging himself to run various errands ashore before the *Steadfast* left port in a few weeks. Straightforward, restful work—almost as though Elie were a kid again, elated that Uncle Simeon had finally trusted him with a navy agent's license and a few clients of his own.

Simeon Benezet's father—Elie's grandfather—had started as a simple slopseller, purveying fabric and ready-made clothing to the Navy and its men. Decades later, that was still the bulk of Benezet & Sons' business, but on a vastly larger scale, with sidelines in a wide array of goods. With Navy paydays few and far between, selling on credit against pay and prize money was the only way to sell in quantity—and the only hope most sailors had of keeping themselves in any comfort.

These days, there were ships where Elie served as unofficial banker to two-thirds of the crew.

His only clients on the *Steadfast,* however, were the men handpicked by Captain Hope from the *Cocksure,* experienced and steady. Payday, bread, and friendly chit-chat combined to put them in good humor. Even better, most of them had long ago sold Elie their small shares in the *Vliegende Draeck* outright, and were in no hurry for the prize settlement.

So Elie avoided thinking about the *Draeck* settlement, just as he avoided looking through the bulkhead windows at the Marine's upright back and musket, or watching for Brine to come striding across the upper deck.

He couldn't help looking when Brine actually appeared at the threshold—usually to fetch something, but once or twice merely to make a sharp-eyed sweep of the vicinity. Which Elie did appreciate, even when it made him lose his place in a sum or a sentence.

Even when Brine opened the door *just* as Elie was saying to the boatswain's mate, "I am begging you to wear a French letter," and sliding the article in question across Brine's chart-table.

Even when Brine laughed.

"Sir, you can't tell me *you* use one of these cursed things!" said the mate.

"I certainly *should* do, if I meant to insert my prick into a perfect stranger," Brine retorted. "But I find a book is easier on my health and my pocketbook. You should try it."

"I d'know, sir… You really put your prick in a book?" The mate made a dubious face, eyes twinkling. "It takes all kinds, and no mistake."

Brine shouted with laughter. "Our coarse talk is making poor Mr. Eleazar blush. Buy the damn condom and put him out of his misery." And he ducked out with a friendly rap on the door jamb.

The mate, who knew Elie was generally unblushing about coarse talk, fought to keep a straight face. "Take heart, sir. He never said he wouldn't insert his prick into a business acquaintance."

Elie rolled his eyes. "I'm insulted by your insinuations," he said perfunctorily, raising his voice to be heard over the mate's guffaws. "Now, will you buy this, or do I have to calculate for you how many times over it would pay for itself in just the first year?"

It was just past four thirty, and Brine still hadn't gone over his account with Elie. Elie was trying to talk the Marine into going in search of him, when a sailor came in and heaved Brine's trunk brazenly onto his shoulders.

Elie blinked. "I—er—ought you—?"

The man barely spared Elie a glance. "Mr. Brine says you're wanted on deck."

Well, that was that. Elie had done his best, and had no choice but to come back another day to confer with Brine. He'd promised to redeem Mr. Lopez's knife from pawn, anyway, and have Mr. Calhoun's watch repaired. He *would* have sent the items by messenger to make more time for the *Vliegende Draeck* accounting, but now...

Brine appeared in the doorway, smiling at him.

Elie, distracted, barely pressed himself against the

bulkhead in time to avoid being hit in the face by the trunk as it went past. "When shall I come back—?" Brine squeezed by him to unhook his ditty-bag.

"Sir, you're sure you don't want me to man a boat for you?" called the trunk-bearer from the doorway.

"No, the Jews' wherry will suit me fine," Brine replied. "I shall be lodging with Mr. Eleazar's family in any case."

3

"You have shore leave?"

Brine glanced at him. "Did my letter not reach you?"

"I'm—behind on my correspondence. Was there anything else important in it?"

"We're leaving without you, Elie!" he heard Samuel bellow. Dazedly, he buckled his pack.

"I can get someone to carry that for you," said Brine.

That jolted him awake. "No, thank you," he said, appalled. Unfortunately, the ship rolled just as he shouldered the pack's weight, and he had to catch himself on the chilly iron muzzle of the great gun. Feh! He spat hastily to ward off bad luck and hurried onto the deck.

Everyone else was already in the wherry, squeezing fore and aft to make space for Brine's trunk, currently being lowered on ropes. "Leaving without me, were you?"

Samuel shrugged unrepentantly.

At least all their packs were lighter now. Elie climbed down without mishap, and the traders waited through the embarrassing profusion of ceremony and saluting and fussing that accompanied Mr. Brine into the boat. Pious old men were less solemn during the procession of the Torah! But Elie reminded himself that these sailors would no doubt find the procession of the Torah absurd in their turn, and strove for toleration.

Brine sat disturbingly close on Elie's narrow plank seat, casting his eyes over the impatient passengers as the boat pushed away from the ship. "The sky's barely pink yet. What's the hurry?"

"Properly, we're meant to stop working and traveling an hour before dark," Elie said. "More to the point, I'd like to wash and shave before the evening service."

Brine grinned. "Now you mention it, you do look a bit raffish." He set his hat in Elie's lap and stood, calling to the waterman, "Can you give her more sail?"

The waterman shrugged. "I'll set her mizzen if you man the jib, sir." Elie didn't bother to puzzle out the stream of terms of art which followed; he watched Brine's sure hands on the rigging instead. The boat plunged and skittered for only a few seconds before she evened out, skimming over the gilded surface of the water.

Brine braced himself against the boom and turned his face into the wind, laughing for pure joy. The sun wasn't low enough to set his hair aflame, but it managed a warm glow. The wind, too, considerately brushed aside his coat-tails to offer Elie an unimpeded view of his arse.

"Any new sandbars since… When was I last here, Mr. Eleazar?"

"July 1811."

Samuel twisted round to raise his eyebrows.

"I have a good memory for numbers," Elie said with dignity.

"Give her a little more, sir," Brine cajoled the skipper.

"This isn't a pilot-boat, young man," the waterman grumbled. "I don't risk her for an extra quarter-knot."

"I'll pay if we damage her." Brine winked at Elie. "I've got prize money coming in."

Elie sat straight up. "Absolutely not. It's not the end of the world if we're late."

Brine laughed. "You don't really think I'll run us aground?"

"Don't waste your breath, Elie," old Mr. Fonseca advised. "You'll never make a sailor understand the value of money."

Elie did not, at present, have a breath to waste. The boat strained for a moment, wobbled, jerked, and ran smoothly for the shore. All at once, it was that handspan of time when the day's autumn blazed red and gold. Each day a year in miniature, and winter coming on…

Days and years alike seemed to begin in promise and hope, and end in a vague sense of failure: *I've wasted another one.* Why did Elie persist in believing he could do better tomorrow, after a lifetime of opposing evidence?

But neither the day nor the year had run out when they touched the shore; Brine had got them home with the sun's lower limb just brushing the roofs of Gosport across the harbor. Now Brine hopped onto the shingle and stood by to assist the traders out. Sailors never *would* believe a landlubber could manage anything to do with boats at all. Yet his polite deference to the older hawkers—quite as if they had been Christians, or gentlemen—warmed Elie.

Elie and Samuel climbed out last. Brine crouched to hold the lightened boat steady. "Thanks for getting us back early," Elie said.

Brine smiled up at him. "Thus, though we cannot make our sun stand still, yet we will make him run."

Elie nearly tripped, lifetime of clambering in and out of boats notwithstanding. He covered it by turning to help drag the boat higher on the beach. The unfamiliar quotation sounded inexplicably intimate—as though Brine had meant *you and I* by that *we.* Elie's imagination, no doubt.

Brine caught at Elie's shoulder for balance as he stood. "Sorry. I haven't been on land since—July 1811, I think you said." Maybe his conviction that the traders needed steadying had only been misguided sympathy, after all—or maybe he was judging them all by Elie's performance today.

Samuel seized a trunk handle, and Elie reluctantly shrugged off Brine's hand to take the other. The sun was setting fast. "I can carry it," Brine protested.

"This will be quicker." Samuel crunched up Broad Street.

Brine wobbled after them. "At least let me hire a porter."

"There's nothing degrading about carrying a trunk," Samuel said. "Whatever they might tell you in the Navy."

Elie swallowed his snicker; Brine looked abashed and uncertain enough already, behind his show of bluff equanimity. He watched his feet as he walked, now and then craning his neck to look up at the buildings lining the street— not so tall as the *Steadfast*'s rigging, but infinitely more opaque. He glanced over his shoulder with every third step, as if to reassure himself that the sea was still there.

He seemed to breathe easier when they passed under King James's Gate and came out along the sea-wall, soldiers scurrying about on the Platform Battery below in preparations for firing their salute to the setting sun. But soon they turned onto the High Street, and thence to streets bounded on all sides by houses and shops.

"We'll be on the Hard soon," Elie promised. The Common

Hard—a coveted address for shopkeepers—fronted the harbor and had its own dock. The Lazaruses' shop, where Samuel sold his silver goods and his brother Morris had an optician's counter in the corner, was a little farther on.

Brine's head swung towards him, startled that Elie had noticed his faint unease. Elie should have kept his mouth shut, instead of discomfiting Brine *and* making it obvious he was vividly aware of Brine's slightest motion, even in the fading light, even out of the corner of his eye.

"Why, I'm all right." Brine's tone suggested Elie must be all about in the head to think otherwise. "I'll be used to everything standing still by tomorrow."

"Forgive me, I forgot officers aren't allowed to be nervous." *Like us cringing Jews,* he barely swallowed. Shit, that had been bitter, and in a few minutes it would be the new year. There went the first lamplighter of the evening with his ladder.

…Mr. Brine showed great coolness and decision…

Officers *weren't* allowed to look nervous, not even when cannonballs were whizzing past their heads, and Elie knew perfectly well why: nerves were catching. He was on edge right now because Brine was.

"I didn't mean to offend," Brine said less blithely, and fell back a pace or two.

A ship was a soap-bubble floating in an enormous tub. Breathe wrong, and it might pop. The Navy told its officers the trick was to make the men believe they didn't need to fret about any of that. Someone was in charge, and *he* knew what he was about.

This brought us perilously near the shore, but Mr. Brine assured me… Even the captain looked to the sailing master when his nerve faltered.

When Elie had been on edge on the *Steadfast*, on edge on the wherry, Brine had smiled at him as if he'd never worried about anything in his life, and tried to solve Elie's problems as best he knew how. And for all Elie had been a bit out of his element on the *Steadfast*—looked at another way, a paid-off frigate *was* his element. Elie was in and out of paid-off ships twice a week sometimes.

Brine hadn't set foot ashore in over two years. He'd spent a scant several months on land, all told, since he turned thirteen. England was supposed to be Brine's home, yet he'd left a ship he knew like the back of his hand, where he was the acknowledged expert on everything, for a place where his only guide, his only glimmer of welcome, was—Elie. A business acquaintance.

"I'm sorry," Elie said as they came out onto the Hard at last. "I shouldn't have snapped at you. Pride goes before a fall."

Brine relaxed a little, looking up from his feet. His attention was a finger stroking down Elie's spine. Feeling ticklish, Elie opened his mouth to make the obvious joke about falling and dropping the trunk.

"I never thought of you as having much pride," Brine said quietly. Quietly for him, anyway—cannon-fire wasn't kind to sailors' hearing. "You always seem to bend like the reed."

What could Elie say to that? Samuel was tactfully silent—or maybe just bored—but he was still far too knowing an audience. They had passed the dockyard gates and turned up Queen Street before Elie said, "So do you. But not *always*."

"Do I?" Brine turned this over. His teeth flashed crookedly as they passed under a lamp. "But we have hearts of oak, eh?"

"It takes pride, I think, to persevere in thankless mathematics without getting sloppy."

He felt Brine's surprise.

Elie tightened his grip on the trunk. He'd never before pointed out the affinity he saw between their work, lest Brine repudiate it. He knew his own calculations weren't so starkly life-and-death. But people relied on him to keep them afloat, nonetheless.

"I thank you," Brine said uncertainly. "Don't I?"

"Yes." Was this ache in Elie's chest sweet, or bitter?

"And here we are!" Samuel pounded on the shop door, adding a piercing whistle for good measure.

His sixteen-year-old daughter, Lottie, opened it. "Hurry up, we'll be late, and Violet Franchetti is saving me a seat—oh! Good evening, Mr. Brine, I forgot you were coming. Welcome."

"Gracious, is that you, Lottie? I've got to call you Miss Lazarus now, I suppose."

"Watch your elbow!" Elie warned.

Samuel dodged a glass case just in time. "Thanks. I've really got to widen this gangway." Lottie nipped around another case to hold open the door to the back of the house, where the family lived.

Brine, following them into the passageway, peered up the narrow, uneven stairs into gathering darkness. "You all go on, I can manage my trunk from here. Thanks for—"

"You really are a very grateful young man," Samuel said in amusement. "But it's bad luck for a lodger to break his neck on your stairs at the new year. Tell the family to go ahead, Lottie. Uncle Elie and I will come as soon as we can."

By the time they'd wrestled the trunk upstairs and deposited it in the empty third-floor room next to Elie's, there was no time to shave. He wiped away as much dirt as he could, hurried into a good suit, and rushed downstairs—then ran back up for his prayerbook.

Erev Rosh Hashanah came only once a year, so Elie tried not to let it slip past in distracted impatience. But Augie Brine came even more rarely, so he only partially succeeded.

It didn't help that Portsmouth's synagogue conducted its services in Yiddish. He spoke the language passably, for it came in handy in the clothing trade, and his uncle Hyam Lazarus (of blessed memory) had been Ashkenazi. But Elie's own parents had both been de naçao, and his London family spoke English and Portuguese at home, seasoned with Dutch and French—a living record of his forebears' search for a safe harbor.

At last the service was over, and Elie walked home with his relatives through the darkened streets, Lottie obligingly translating some of the rabbi's more pointed remarks, and bringing him up-to-date on the intricate community squabbles behind them.

They made quite a little procession, all told, even now that a few of his other cousins had peeled off towards their own homes. His mother's sister, Hava Lazarus, was palpably the center of the group. Aunt Hava was still handsome at fifty-six, with dramatic wings of silver in her dark hair and a deep red pelisse that showed off her honey complexion. Her stately aquilinity grew more pronounced with age—a phenomenon Elie observed with delight, as it gave him hope for his own profile, whose curve was at present more hinted at than asserted.

Samuel Lazarus walked with his wife, Leah, a stocky woman with auburn hair and a kind of angular, unvarnished beauty. Their children—Lottie, Zachariah, Kaatje, and Hyam—ranged in age from sixteen to seven.

Aunt Hava's younger son Morris, whose wife had stayed home with the baby, bore two-year-old Aaron on his shoulders, while Elie followed with Gracia, just turned three.

Was it his imagination that Gracia was heavier than she'd been when Elie left for Rye Bay just a few weeks ago? And her new favorite game was to put her hands over his eyes while he was walking. Still, it was a short walk from the synagogue to the Lazarus house, and Elie had to stay her favorite uncle somehow. He worried now and then that the younger children would forget him during one of his frequent absences, though it hadn't happened yet.

Elie lived above the Lazarus shop about a third of his time, and another half with his mother in the City of London, where he could easily visit the Bank of England, the Thames docks, the Admiralty Office, several Royal shipyards, and most of Uncle Simeon's warehouses and counting-houses. In between, he traveled wherever Benezet & Sons business took him— other ports and Royal dockyards, the northern manufacturing towns, even the occasional journey to Rotterdam or Antwerp, when the war didn't make it impossible.

Elie felt a pang. Did his mother envy Aunt Hava, surrounded by her little dynasty? Was there loneliness behind her constant refrain of *When are you going to give me grandchildren, Elie?* When mãe had married the youngest Benezet brother, of the rising firm Benezet & Benezet, it had seemed a much finer match than her sister's to Hyam Lazarus. But Elie's father had died young, leaving his wife with a small son to raise alone, dependent on Uncle Simeon's generosity—however considerable that generosity had been. Did mãe have regrets?

He should have sent her a note this morning, wishing her a sweet new year. Of course he'd written her a long letter on the boat from Rye, with as much of Jael's news as could be safely committed to paper, but—

"I'm taller than you, tateh!" Gracia told Morris, giggling.

"Ah, everybody's taller than me," Morris said without rancor.

"Mameh's taller than you too!"

Morris smiled. "Your mameh is like to a palm tree," he said, "and her eyes are like the fishpools of Heshbon."

Gracia laughed so hard that Elie had to put her down on the shop's doorstep, feeling another sharp pang as she darted away. "It seems like yesterday I was carrying *you* on my shoulders," he told twelve-year-old Zach, who already towered over the entire family.

"You still can, if you like," Zach said magnanimously.

As they trooped through the darkened shop, someone up ahead opened the door to the family living quarters, letting in light and sound. Somewhere nearby, Brine was singing "Heart of Oak," and Elie forgot what he had been going to say.

"They swear they'll invade us, these terrible foes,
They frighten our women, our children, and beaus;
But should their flat bottoms in darkness get o'er,
Still Britons they'll find to receive them on shore!"

Luckily, Zach had already been carried away by the current as they all poured noisily into the bright, warm kitchen, where

Brine had evidently been enlisted to distract little Reuben while Morris's wife, Rebecca, sliced apples. He held the baby very gingerly, and looked entirely out of his depth.

"Tateh said your eyes were like fish, mameh!"

Rebecca laughed. "Well, you tell your tateh from me that his hair is like a flock of goats."

Elie went to Brine, meaning to take the baby off his hands—but couldn't resist letting him suffer just a bit longer.

Casting him a reproachful look, Brine began the chorus. "'Heart of oak are our ships, heart of oak are our men!'" The first part of this was mostly literal, the best ships being built from the oak tree's dense heartwood. "'We always are ready—'"

"Are you teaching my nephew bawdy songs?"

Rattled, Brine cut off. "Of course not, I'd never—"

Elie grinned at him. "The French are menacing your beaux but, in the dark, your enemy's bottoms succumb to English hardwood?"

Brine's eyes glinted. "You might have grasped the stick by the wrong end, there." Was Elie imagining that he said it…flirtatiously?

Elie shouldn't be flirting with Brine in the first place. Penitent, he pried the baby from Brine's inexpert grasp.

Brine sagged in relief. "Thanks. If you drop a sextant, you might be able to keep using it afterwards."

"Babies are sturdier than you'd think. Aren't you, Ru-ru?" Elie tickled Reuben's tummy with his nose. The baby seized the opportunity to knock his hat onto the floor. "I let you do that."

Rebecca patted Brine on the shoulder as she wove between them with the tray of apples. "You'll learn. It's good practice for when you're married."

At that, Brine looked nearly as queasy as Elie felt. The future Mrs. Brine would have her work cut out, raising children with him. Still, the prize money would pay for a nursemaid.

And maybe Brine was just tired. Oh, he was plainly making efforts to be sociable and well-mannered, wearing his dress uniform and proposing Friday's bloodthirsty wardroom toast after the Kiddush. But by the time Zach herded the younger children into the next room and dinner began, he was looking as worn as the uniform. He ate methodically, as if lading his stomach for a long voyage, licking the last drops of honey from his fingers—incidentally inspiring very bawdy thoughts about the enthusiastic reception Elie's bottom would give said fingers.

Lottie, seeming oblivious both to Brine's fatigue and to his good looks, peppered him ruthlessly with technical questions about *The Seaman's Guide and Coaster's Companion*, which she'd recently borrowed from Elie's stores.

"Thank goodness an expert has arrived," Elie remarked. "The poor girl tried to ask *me* all this yesterday."

Brine smiled and produced a credible lecture on the idiosyncratic behavior of the waters in Rye Bay, quite exploding the popular misconception that the very high tides were due to the Channel and North Sea tides meeting there. But he was less fluent on less familiar topics, and the third time he began answering a question about his impending nuptials only to trail off, fumbling for an elusive word, he turned to Elie.

"What about you, Mr. Eleazar? I always think I'll come back to find you married, but..." He waved a hand vaguely. "I don't."

"An excellent question, sir." Aunt Hava shook her head, earrings wobbling. "Maybe this year. A nice, handsome boy who earns a good living, twenty-six and not married when so many Jewish girls want husbands. It's a shonde."

"A disgrace," Elie translated. Brine winced.

"Not *all* Jewish girls want husbands," muttered Lottie—too quietly for her grandmother to hear.

Not for the first time, Elie wondered if his niece might be uninterested in marriage for the same reason he was. Not for the first time, he wondered if he should try to talk to her about it. But it was such a delicate subject, and Lottie could be a chatterbox. Surely a pronounced reluctance to marry wasn't so uncommon in sixteen-year-old girls as all that. Although if she was really as immune to Brine's palpable attractions as she appeared…

"Give Elie another year, mamã," Morris said slyly. "Just until Jael Collavecchia and her fortune are out of mourning."

Brine's eyebrows went up. "Who?"

"A childhood friend, *very* recently widowed." Elie gave Morris a pointed look. "I've spent the last few weeks in Rye Bay sorting out her affairs, which is why I didn't get your letter, Brine."

"Ah. Is she pretty?"

"A great beauty," Aunt Hava said. "A blonde. She and Elie made such a striking pair, always laughing together. Her father supplied straw hats for the Benezets. Everyone said what a fine match it would be."

"If by 'everyone' you mean my own relations," Elie said. "Impartial observers could admit that I was only one of many dark-haired men in London."

Leah sniffed. "Yes, the Collavecchias thought they could

do better. Jael must be sorry she didn't take Elie."

"That's enough," Elie said firmly, more on principle than out of any expectation of being listened to. "Jael sold us her father's business at a good price after he died, and no one could have guessed that Palethorp would be…" He trailed off, not wanting to be indiscreet about Jael's private misfortunes. Nor was he exactly *eager* to list the inadequacies of a navy agent as suitor to a beautiful heiress, even if they must be obvious to everyone. "It was six years ago. Let it alone."

"Still, Dividend Day at the Bank of England is coming up in a couple of weeks," Rebecca said. "It couldn't hurt to deliver her money yourself."

Elie ignored this. Talk was cheap, and Jael herself was in no danger of misunderstanding his intentions, even if he did visit her in Brighton to see how she was getting on. Her heart was already set on her daughter's governess, anyway.

"Marry in haste, repent at leisure," Lottie said sharply. "Maybe Lady Palethorp would rather collect her own dividends. Ladies can, can't they, Uncle Elie?"

"Yes, they—"

"What haste?" Morris said. "It's not haste to pay a visit. Besides, she's known him forever. She can trust him not to try to take her money like Palethorp. Elie's more likely to present her with a receipt on carbonic paper every time he buys a new suit."

"So…once every three years?" Aunt Hava teased.

Elie laughed, but he caught Brine self-consciously fingering his threadbare lapel. Elie knew exactly when he'd last bought a new suit: at his promotion to master in 1807, thankfully just *after* the Admiralty changed all the warrant officers' uniforms. Had six years really passed since then? It didn't seem so long.

"I don't see any great advantage in waiting ages to marry." Leah twinkled knowingly at Brine. "I'm sure your own bride must be growing impatient, sir."

Brine stiffened. "I have stood ready to marry her all along," he asserted. "But—" His shoulders slumped. "Oh, likely you're right. This last birthday rather sobered me. So many men in my profession never turn thirty at all, and here I've been living as though I had all the time in the world. Still, as a single woman, Miss Turner can draw part of her late father's pension, so until my own income—"

"I meant no criticism, Mr. Brine!" Leah protested. "Unless it was of the Prize Court's inefficiency." She gave her husband a laughing look. "But marriage does have its perquisites."

"Mamã!" Lottie broke in, looking ready to sink with embarrassment. "We *know* what you meant, you needn't explain it. I am so sorry, Mr. Brine."

Brine finally dredged up a genuine-sounding laugh. "No need to apologize. I thank you, Mrs. Samuel, for the kind compliment to myself."

"Well, better late than never," Aunt Hava said comfortingly, and glanced at Elie.

Elie felt sad, suddenly. This would be the rest of his life. No success or accomplishments would ever rate as high as a wife and children. Elie could bring Benezet & Sons a share in the capture of another *Hermione* (a prize so rich even ordinary seamen had received £480 apiece), he could arrive at a holiday dinner dripping in silk and diamonds, and his family would say, *Perhaps now you'll finally settle down!* He could trip gaily home from the counting-house, warbling like a skylark for the sheer joy of living, and they'd say, *You must be so lonely, Elie. Wouldn't you like someone to come home to at night?*

And then Elie felt even sadder, because he *would* like someone to come home to. The man sitting next to him flirting politely with his cousin's wife, in fact.

Of course a sailor didn't wait for you at home. Still, there'd be memories to cherish, and visits to eagerly anticipate, and letters to reread while you ate at your desk, before you bound them up in a velvet ribbon and slid them back into their pigeonhole.

Brine wrote droll, chatty letters to his business acquaintances. What would his love letters be like?

Elie shoved a piece of challah and honey into his mouth, as if that could quell his hunger.

4

SATURDAY

FIRST DAY OF ROSH HASHANAH

Traditional wardroom toast:
"Wives and sweethearts—may they never meet!"

B rine had gone to bed early, and he must have slept late too, since he was—of course—shaving shirtless by the window when Elie returned from the morning service. His clothes were laid out on the bed; as yet, he wore only loose white trousers laced at the small of his back, just tightly enough to keep them clinging to his hipbones. The noon light caught the tips of his hair—all of it, forearms and chest and belly—outlining him in gold leaf like the best illuminated manuscript in the world.

Elie had meant to walk swiftly onward, but Brine turned towards his footsteps. "I'd almost forgotten the glorious luxury of hot water." He wiped away the last traces of soap with a steaming towel. "Ahhh, if that isn't a sweet beginning to the year… Do you have to go back this afternoon? I thought you might come with me to the baths."

Elie pantomimed offense. "Are you saying I stink?"

Brine grinned, crooked teeth flashing. "If I say yes, will you come?" Had Elie walked into a Christian parable about pleasures of the flesh tempting a believer from the path?

Fortunately, he wasn't Christian. He hastily calculated the earliest service he could miss. Today would be too obvious; his family would gossip. He wouldn't mind shirking the binding of Isaac and the prayer for the Royal Family tomorrow morning, but he'd like to hear the first blowing of the shofar, postponed because today was the Sabbath… "I could go tomorrow afternoon. Oh, drat, the bathing-house is closed on Sundays."

"Monday morning?"

"That's a fast day; too much hot steam and I'd probably swoon in your arms."

The grin flashed again. "I'll risk it."

Elie pulled himself together. "Probably best not. Would you wait for Tuesday? No, that's absurd. Go without me."

Brine's jaw dropped. "Are you saying *I* stink?"

"If I say no, will you wait?"

Brine laughed. "I'll go today *and* Tuesday, how's that? The first bath will probably just soften up the grime, anyway." His gaze fell. "You couldn't see your way clear to loaning me another couple of crowns, could you?"

Elie dropped out of someone else's parable and into his own life with a thud. Bad enough he was coveting somebody else's bridegroom, but he was supposed to do the blasted prize accounting Tuesday.

Still, the baths couldn't take more than an hour or two. He thought better when he was clean. "I can loan you three," he said. "I'm not really supposed to handle money on a holiday, but come along and you can take it yourself from my purse."

"Isn't that cheating?"

"I care about the *spirit* of the Law," Elie said. "But if you want to get anything done in this world, you need a certain comfort with loopholes. I'm sure you've noticed that yourself."

"Yes," Brine said in surprise. "I just thought you were—pious, I suppose."

Elie bit his lip. Surely Brine wasn't truly interested in Elie's theological opinions? Elie rarely devoted much thought to them himself, and at the moment Brine's torso seemed to demand his full attention.

"Sorry," Brine said. "It's none of my business. Let me put on a shirt so you can give—so I can take the money and stop pestering you." Passing over shirt and braces, he pulled on a striped Guernsey frock and tucked it into his trousers. Somehow the drape of the thin, clinging knit made the points of Brine's nipples *more* prominent. Or was it the narrow blue stripes deforming around them that drew the eye so unerringly?

Elie dragged his eyes back up to Brine's chastened face, and realized Brine thought he was silent because he was offended. "I ask personal questions for a living," he said. "Please don't apologize. You can ask. The answer's just complicated and dull."

"*I'm* not in a hurry," Brine said. He trailed after Elie to his room, looking about with idle curiosity.

After pointing out the drawer with his purse in it, Elie looked too, hoping nothing too revealing was in view—then felt curiously deflated, for the room could not have revealed anything about him at all. The iron bed, old carved clothespress, and other furniture were all Aunt Hava's. Various cousins in the metalworking trades had given him the monogrammed razor and mirror, and the only book on display was a novel Jael had talked him into reading, since his small collection of guidebooks had mysteriously migrated to Lottie's room during a recent absence.

Everything else, Elie had let clients talk him into accepting in lieu of payment, right down to the cracked whale on the mantel, carved from a whale's tooth, and the silhouette portrait of someone else's bewigged grandmother.

Elie looked down at himself. His quilted waistcoat had belonged to a ship's carpenter leaving the North Sea for the Mediterranean.

Elie liked his things. That grinning little whale had had its wounds on the Glorious First of June. It would have been absurd to spend good money on new things he wouldn't like any better, and this made it easier to let the room to boarders when Elie was away.

But for a moment, all Elie could see was that he and his things were equally surplus. They were what other people had decided not to keep.

Brine counted out three crowns into his palm and showed them to Elie. "Make sure you add it to my account."

"I will," Elie lied. But even with cash in hand, Brine lingered.

Maybe all Elie would ever have of Brine were notes dashed off between more pressing duties, and leftover moments between tours of duty and visits to his wife. Was that a reason to rush through them, and make them less than they were? Was it a reason for Elie to make *himself* less than he was, to fit more neatly into the gaps and margins? Brine wasn't in a hurry.

"The spirit of the Sabbath is that—that there's something holy in the world, more than our human bustle and business," he began haltingly. "That there's more to each of us than the work we do and the things we make. That it's all right to slow down and just *be*. If I make you wait till tomorrow for your bath, that isn't holy, it's red tape."

Brine wandered to the window and leaned on the sill, listening attentively. His bare feet and the slight cock of his hip were obscene poems in some Classical language Elie had never learned.

"You only think I'm pious because I try not to bend the rules too much with Gentiles watching," he went on, realizing just how much he *had* sanded off his sharp corners to slide smoothly in and out of Brine's life. Maybe Brine wouldn't like him anymore, once Elie said what he really thought. "If I do, you always seem to think it means more than it does. That I'm underhanded, or that—that your rules are the only ones that matter, after all."

No sign of offense in Brine's face yet. He only ran his thumb pensively over his mouth, one way and then the other, scattering Elie's thoughts.

"It's as though, if I handle a few coins one Saturday," Elie managed, "then I have no right to say I won't draft a contract next Saturday, and neither has anyone else. I can't seem to explain that I believe a humane law must be flexible, without a Gentile taking it to mean that I don't believe anything at all. But you don't furl every sail on a Sunday, and somehow that doesn't shake Christianity to its foundations. Hillel—one of our Sages—said, 'What you'd hate if someone did it to you, don't do to them. That's the whole Torah; the rest is exegesis.'"

"I like that," Brine said. "It's the kind of philosophy you can live in comfortably." He sighed. "Sarah can be a bit of a stickler for the forms of things." His eyes swept the room glumly. "This looks so comfortable and easy. I hope she doesn't make me throw away all my old things and buy new." He rolled his shoulders, and then glanced at Elie, eyes crinkling. "It would be a windfall for you, anyway. Thanks for pretending not to notice the sorry state of my dress coat last night."

Elie dismissed this with a shrug.

"A new undress coat wouldn't hurt either, frankly. But I've been putting it off because then I won't be able to move my arms for six months."

"We'll tell the tailor to cut the sleeves loose."

Brine's face brightened. "You think that would be all right?"

Elie felt a pang. "I can't pretend to speak for the wardroom. But it looked to me like they respect you on the *Steadfast* in the coat you have."

"They do, don't they?" This smile was shyer than usual. "But—you don't think—I don't want my wife to be…" The smile faded. "I don't want to embarrass her."

It felt self-serving to say this. Yet not to say it was surely a dereliction of duty. "If you don't *want* to marry Miss Turner…" Elie began in fear and trembling.

"She's a wonderful woman," Brine said at once, forcefully. "God. I'd better take care or I'll become one of those men who thinks it's witty to call his wife Xanthippe or a whither-go-ye."

Whither-go-ye Elie had heard. The joke, to use the term loosely, was that wives sometimes thought themselves entitled to inquire where their husbands were going when they left home. "Xanthippe?"

"Socrates's wife. She had a reputation as a scold."

"Ah." Elie couldn't think of anything else to say. "I suppose we should go down to dinner."

"Had I better put on my dress uniform again?" Brine said without enthusiasm. "I'd hate to show your aunt any disrespect."

"Enh, this isn't London. Just put on a coat." *And I won't object if you leave your throat bare,* he thought, trying not to lose himself in the hollow of Brine's collarbone.

Brine stripped off his Guernsey and went bare-chested to dig in his trunk. Surfacing with his plain coat, he caught Elie's blank expression. "Sorry, after the North Sea everything feels like the tropics. You're billing me for all this coal, aren't you?"

"Every lump," Elie lied, having noticed that if he explained that Brine's coal was included in his board, Brine would quietly stint himself to protect Aunt Hava's profits. The room did feel like the tropics. Why was the hair at Brine's underarms so attractive? It was like—the opposite of a reminder of mortality. As if Elie was suddenly remembering that handsome naked men weren't all made of marble and alabaster. That Brine was flesh and blood, and so was he.

Just then, Lottie clattered up the stairs. "Vó says—" She froze in the doorway. "Oh dear."

Brine turned round, coat in hand, and froze likewise. "Lottie! I—ahem." He snatched his shirt off the bed and dove into it. "I wasn't expecting you. That is, of course it's your house, I only—"

"It was my fault, Mr. Brine, I beg your pardon." Lottie looked mortified. "I really didn't mean to stare. I hope I haven't embarrassed you."

Brine laughed. "Not at all, Miss Lazarus." He winked at her. "What do you think, does my bride have reason to be impatient?"

Lottie tried to look very worldly and jaded while turning bright red. "Vó says dinner's ready," she said in dignified tones, and whisked herself away.

Elie cleared his throat, absolutely hating that he had to say this. "Listen, Brine, Lottie isn't… Don't touch her. Even if she stares at you. If I find you have, I…"

Brine looked as if Elie had struck him. "I wouldn't seduce your niece. Christ. I just didn't want her to think she'd offended me."

Elie let out his breath. "I'm sorry. It's not—anything you've done, yourself. I've just seen a lot of sailors on leave. Plenty of men wouldn't see any harm… A sixteen-year-old girl, if she were willing…" And some people thought everything in a Jewish home was for sale.

Brine looked at the plain coat in his hands, and went back to his trunk and traded it for his dress uniform after all. "I remember when you sold me my first bicorne, and she wanted to try it on," he said sadly. "We had to stuff the crown with paper to keep it from covering half her face. I've remembered it all this time, and now I come back and she's two feet taller and you don't even know me well enough to…"

"I'm sorry," Elie said miserably. "My manners are atrocious."

Brine's jaw tightened. "Of course the problem isn't your *manners*. Of course you're only trying to do right by—by everyone. You haven't got any reason to trust my word. I know I'm just one of a parade of your clients who rent this room. But I promise you, you won't ever need to sell me a French letter. And I—I care about—" His shoulders slumped. "I care about your family," he muttered, rubbing at his forehead.

Elie didn't know how to answer. *My family cares about you too* was probably an exaggeration, while *You're my favorite client* was both absurd understatement and too close to a declaration to be safely voiced. He watched Brine fit his black stock over his throat and buckle it at the nape of his neck. He watched him do up all eight buttons of his white waistcoat.

"I'm sorry," Elie repeated at last. "If I don't know you well, it's due to circumstance, and not—inclination."

Brine gave him a tiny, rueful half-smile as he shrugged into his coat. "Thanks."

"They should have given you an epaulet," he blurted out. "It's an insult they gave the lieutenants one, and not you."

Brine laughed, shoulders relaxing. For a second Elie was relieved, and then he remembered that Brine had done the same for Lottie: *I just didn't want her to think she'd offended me.* "Don't wish an epaulet on me! If you could see the lieutenants sweating and praying every time they unwrap them, for fear they've crimped a bullion— I *could* have taken the lieutenant's exam, if I'd wanted to idle on half-pay in an epaulet instead of—" He cut himself off.

"Working without one," Elie finished for him.

Brine's eyes glinted at him, bright as gold braid. "I remembered I shouldn't be bitter at Rosh Hashanah."

Hearing his broad, sturdy accent wrapped around the holiday's name made Elie's belly tighten. "Being a gentleman is overrated," he said, and then was horrified at himself. "Not that you aren't one! I'd never— I really didn't mean that. Of course you are." Actually, Elie had no idea one way or the other and couldn't have cared less, but he knew it mattered very much to Brine. "I forgot myself."

"No," Brine said, after a pause. "At sea, it's either be a gentleman or be odd man out in the wardroom. And odd man out, when you're a dot on the ocean, is nowhere. I don't mean to make the officers sound like snobs. There's plenty didn't start out any higher than me, and on a good ship they're generous and willing to welcome you, irrespective of accents and epaulets. It's easier to let yourself be welcomed. But on shore, I remember the world of men is wide." He checked the fall of his cuffs, and slipped on his buckled shoes. For a second, their eyes met. "I know you only ever meant to welcome me," he said quietly. "And you have." He tugged at his collar. "Damn, I'm sweating already. The North Sea has ruined me for ordinary weather."

Elie *really* couldn't think of anything to say to all that, so he tried for a frank, manly hand on Brine's shoulder. But as soon as he felt Brine's muscles under his palm, the contact seemed guiltily insinuating. He gave up and led the way downstairs.

The wardroom's Saturday toast, Elie knew, was *To wives and sweethearts—may they never meet!* Brine raised his glass, then glanced at Elie and took a hasty swig instead. Too hasty— he choked just as Elie sent him a grateful smile for trying to be proper around Lottie.

Poor Brine spent the next several minutes reassuring Aunt Hava that he was quite well—No, there hadn't been a bone in her fish—Yes, he was always careful eating fish—She was right, it was far too easy to scratch your throat if you weren't careful.

Elie lay in bed, planning out the *Vliegende Draeck* accounting. First he had to comb through his recent mail for any fresh documents related to the case. Then he had to collate every account, invoice, and bill of sale. That done, he could pay outstanding fees, replace missing receipts, and dun any late-paying buyers.

That last probably did mean a visit to the thrice-cursed Ordnance Board.

The prize system was intended to encourage industry and daring in the Navy—and to supplement the low pay, which even after wartime increases was far below what a man could earn on a merchant ship. But delay and red tape were the hallmark of successful bureaucracies like the Royal Navy. Only once a captured ship was ruled lawful prize by a Prize Court could it and its cargo be sold—and that was only the beginning.

Oh, a victorious captain and crew might receive their prize and bounty money quickly on a French warship captured by a single British frigate. But legal complexities multiplied if more than one admiral had a claim to being the British captain's commanding officer, or if another Royal Navy ship had been within sight of the capture, or even if the size of the enemy crew was disputed.

Cases like the *Vliegende Draeck*'s could drag on even longer, for the *Draeck* was no warship, but a merchantman accused of transporting contraband—an elastic category, perennially debated in lawsuits and insurance policies.

Naturally one didn't wish the Royal Navy to devolve into a pirate fleet, and the *Draeck*'s Dutch owners had been within their rights to file an appeal and seek damages for lost profits. But Elie couldn't help wishing they had saved their money and spared him some of the four or five solid inches of paper now sitting on his desk.

And that file was only the financial side of the case! The affidavits and briefs were for the prize agent to worry about, thank Heaven. (Prize agents weren't required to be attorneys, but it certainly helped—one reason they were Gentiles almost to a man, the legal profession being closed to Jews.)

Still, the *Draeck* case was settled now. All that remained was for Elie to finish the accounting.

…Well, and then he had to make a final audit of the Prize List. Once he'd struck the names of any recent deserters from the *Cocksure*'s crew, he could calculate the precise number of shares in each eighth and the value of each. And after that, he had to make an attested copy of his results for the Admiralty Court's public register, to give interested parties a chance to examine them.

He should get up and take a few notes. But it was cold and pitch dark, the moon still new. Lighting a candle would take ages. Better to get a good night's sleep and be fresh tomorrow.

Shit, and he'd have to read though the final judgment to make sure it upheld an earlier decision barring HMS *Audacious* from a share in the prize, as the fog had been too thick for her to be within sight of the action…

There was no strict limit for when the final accounts had to be submitted, he reminded himself. The statute read only "within a reasonable period of time"—a turn of phrase as elastic as "contraband," lending itself equally to abuse by the unscrupulous and to giving Elie palpitations when in a self-recriminating mood.

He thought of the prayer he'd said today in synagogue: *The truth is that You alone are lawyer, judge, and witness. You transcribe and stamp, You tally and keep accounts. You remember what's been forgotten. You will open the record-book and it will all be read out, and every man's signature will be in it, in his own hand…*

When HaShem audited Elie's books, what would He think of them? When He saw how Elie had falsified Brine's account, would He say *Anonymous charity is a mitzvah*, or *I'm revoking your license for fraud*?

Elie would support Brine openly if he could. But they weren't family, *couldn't* be family. The only thing Brine and the rest of the world wouldn't think awfully peculiar was to extend him as much credit as Elie could afford, and not dun him.

He hadn't planned to hide it from Brine, at first. At first he hadn't *planned* it at all. He'd been eighteen and bashful and willing to let a handsome new client outrun his income by five or ten pounds in the vague hope of thanks and a smile, that was all. He'd daydreamed, at best, of Brine realizing Elie could be squeezed and devoting a few extra minutes to cozening him, next time he was in port. Most sailors treated their navy agents like enemy shipping: anything they could get away with seizing was lawful prize.

And then all of a sudden Elie had been inundated with letters like: *I send herewith several certificates for pilotage due me, endorsed to you for redemption at the Office of the Commissioners of the Navy, viz.—*

(Here followed a list of enclosures in precise columns.)

I beg you will apply this to my account, which I believe brings my debt to 2 · 15 · —. You will inform me if I mistake. Your humble servant, &c., Julius Pickle (an old Salt).

P.S. — The pig you procured for me was excellent eating and I received many compliments upon him.

Beneath this Brine had doodled his beloved detached-escapement pocket watch above the motto *ARSE LONGA, VITA BREVIS*. To its left was a grinning piglet, captioned *Yesterday*, and to its right a plate of chops labeled *Today*.

Elie groaned and buried his face in his pillow. It wasn't *fair* for Brine to be so darling.

He should skip synagogue tomorrow and go straight to the counting-house. But Samuel would come and drag him out by his ear, and Brine... Brine would think Elie was inordinately conscientious, when the exact opposite was true. Elie rolled over and tried to sleep.

There was a clatter from the next room, followed by an exclamation of pain, and then cursing.

"Brine? Are you well?"

"Perfectly well, sorry!" Brine called back, too brightly and too loud, just as Reuben started wailing downstairs. "...*Shit*."

Elie sighed. It took a slight expenditure of will to throw back the covers. He lay shivering a moment—sat up—shivered another moment—and ducked through the bedcurtains.

5

The baby was still shrieking when he knocked on Brine's door a few minutes later.

"…Come."

Brine sat sullenly on the edge of his bed, pressing a bloody handkerchief to his foot. Despite the chill, he wore no stockings with his smallclothes, and his Guernsey had the sleeves rolled up. "It's nothing—" he began, and then Elie's dressing gown appeared to rob him of the power of speech.

Elie sighed so heavily he nearly extinguished his candle. His mother had quilted him the garment out of six worn-out gowns in six bright colors and patterns, and finished it with a broad astrakhan collar and obsolete flag-officers' buttons. "How bad's the cut?"

Brine glared at his foot. "The *cut* is nothing. I broke my spectacles."

Elie's eyebrows went up. "Nothing, I see. And which part of your spectacles went into your foot, exactly? The wire? The glass? The—"

"I'm sorry I woke the baby." Brine wrapped the kerchief around his foot and began to tie it off.

Elie prayed for patience. "Here, hold this." He thrust the candle into Brine's startled hands and swiftly confiscated the kerchief. "Is there any glass still in the cut?" He'd have liked to think even a naval officer wouldn't be that foolhardy, but he examined the cut himself despite Brine's headshake. The wound was small, but anything could get infected, and there was always tetanus… "Where are the eyeglasses?"

Brine produced them: a cracked lens and bent frame, but not notably bloodstained.

"How deep is it?" He gave Brine an admonitory look. "The truth, now."

"Not deep."

Elie narrowed his eyes. Brine gazed guilelessly back, laughing at him. Elie turned away, face hot. "Good. I'll be right back."

Brine laughed again when Elie carried in his portable medicine chest. "Is there any emergency you're unequipped for?"

"I've been trying to sell it for months, but there are only so many surgeons kitting out." Elie sat next to him, taking out a roll of lint bandage and a small bottle. "And the mass of Englishmen are shockingly indifferent to their health," he added pointedly.

This close, Brine smelled of cardamom and orange peel. Shouldn't that be pleasant and sweet, like an expensive biscuit? Instead, Elie thought of wine-merchant words: *racy, ripe, full-bodied, generous.* He hurried to twist off the bottle cap.

Brine wrinkled his nose. "Ugh, not vinegar!"

"Be a man," Elie told him, and didn't know whether to laugh or weep when Brine took the joking rebuke seriously, setting his jaw and staring bravely into the middle distance. Elie cupped his foot in one hand, and wiped the cut with the other.

Brine's breath left his nostrils in a sharp little puff, only audible because Elie was so close. He'd bathed today; the skin against Elie's palm was thin and clean and soft. His calf was perfect, its hair thick and wiry. Elie could feel Brine's body relax when the baby's crying began to abate. It was all horribly intimate.

No it isn't, Elie told himself. *Imagine you're his ship's surgeon, not his wife.* "Who's the *Steadfast*'s surgeon, again?"

"Thomas Galway, why?"

So I can speculate as to whether he's also in love with you. "Just tired and rambling."

"Sorry I woke you."

"You didn't. Hold the bandage while I cut the sticking plaster."

Brine set the candle on the nightstand and obeyed. "Sorry I'm useless."

"What? You aren't—"

"On land, I am. Strange to remember I was born landlocked." Brine shook his head. "Even as a little boy, all I cared about were the boats on the Birmingham canal. My poor father—he was a civil engineer, you remember. He encouraged me at first—hoped maybe I'd design locks one day. Instead I made friends with every visitor I could, until I hit on a toll collector with a brother-in-law at sea and talked my way into a midshipman's berth. My mother wept, and my father told me the Navy was a brutal life, and I was a young fool who'd never even seen the sea and hadn't the faintest idea what I was letting myself in for. But I've never regretted it." He poked at his cut, wincing. "You know, I keep thinking about what you said about the Sabbath. That a man is more than the work he does. But—I'm on good terms with myself when I'm working. I'm a marvel at spherical trigonometry and making sure Mr. Shoemaker doesn't take more than his mess's share of grog.

Put me ashore, and I don't know what's left of any value. I can't even walk a straight line with everything so bloody *still.*"

Elie settled for a sympathetic noise here and there as he applied the sticking plaster. Brine seemed to have more to get off his chest, and *You're a marvel all the time* might be…unsubtle.

"We live like fish in a barrel on the *Steadfast,* until I'd walk over hot coals for a true day of rest. Just a little peace and quiet and elbow room. And now I can't see or hear or feel *anything,* and my thoughts seem loud enough to be heard outside my head." Brine traced the bandage's edge with his thumb. "I got up to open the shutters and see if there were any stars out. I hate the new moon. Lunar altitudes are so much easier than two stars, and—" His lips tightened. "And I can't read the Nautical Almanac on a moonless night anymore, even with my spectacles. I'll have to borrow more money from you to fix the damn things. There's another talent, I suppose— borrowing your money. I'm good at that."

"Enh." Elie shrugged. "You could be better at it. I wouldn't mind."

"Of course you would," Brine said tiredly. "But thanks. For everything."

"Morris made those glasses. He'll fix them for you. Just don't let him sell you anything else while he's doing it. Anything you don't want, anyway." He set Brine's foot down, resisting the urge to pat it first. "Sailors are famous for finding shore life rather a shock. Don't take it so much to heart. Would it cheer you up to teach me spherical trigonometry and see how hopeless I am at it?"

"Don't be coy, Mr. Eleazar, you'd be a prodigy." Mouth curving, he flicked one of Elie's gilt buttons. "You didn't tell me you were promoted. I'd have sent my congratulations."

"We were supposed to return the lot to be melted down, but my mother liked them." The button was between Brine's index and middle finger now, his thumb tracing the raised laurel wreath. His wrist was at once sturdy and delicate—and tanned to the elbow, drat him, why didn't he ever wear enough *clothes*? "Aren't you cold?"

Brine released the button to tweak Elie's astrakhan collar. "Not as cold as you, evidently." His hand fell. "You can go back to bed. I don't think amputation will be necessary."

Elie shrugged. "Do you want company?"

"Your company, Mr. Eleazar? Need you ask?" He said it in that warm, teasing way that made it unclear whether he was joking.

I believe the word you want is "flirting," Elie's brain offered, probably trying to be helpful.

But what if Brine *was* flirting? People did flirt, just as people called strangers "my dear" and signed all their business letters *your devoted servant.* It almost never meant anything, which was how you got away with it when you did mean something.

When, for example, you were writing a business letter to Augustus Brine and hoping your meaning could somehow transmit itself to the ink through your fingers, to imbue the paper with the depth and fervency of your devotion and your desire to be of service.

Brine wrapped himself in his voluminous boat cloak and sat cross-legged on the bed. "Come inside the curtains. It will be warm in a minute."

Elie pulled his feet up and Brine drew the curtains, plunging them into darkness. There was no way to know how close any part of Brine's body might be to any part of his. Elie's imagination began cataloguing possibilities, then swiftly leapt to impossibilities:

Brine's feet grazing his thigh.

Brine's feet in his lap.

Brine's head in his lap.

Brine's mouth on his cock.

This had to stop. "I could try to—" Elie blurted out desperately.

"About my last letter—" Brine began at the same time. "Sorry, you were saying?"

"I could try to find a house along the sea wall for you and Mrs. Brine, if you mean to live in Portsmouth."

The darkness and silence felt so absolute that Elie understood Brine's *My thoughts are loud enough to be heard outside my head.*

"You'd better ask Sarah," Brine said at last. "No sense choosing a house to suit me when I'll barely live in it."

Elie had, up to now, avoided asking Sarah Turner much of anything. He had avoided meeting her with still more energy. Firstly, because Brine's engagement was of such long standing that, in the absence of a corporeal bride, it had been all too easy to imagine it as immaterial, insignificant—very nearly a legal fiction.

Secondly, because whenever Elie *had* exchanged a letter with Miss Turner (usually about her care of Brine's declining parents and, later, their funerals), he'd been left with the distinct impression that she didn't like him.

Still, he might be mistaken. Her brevity—overlaid so transparently and perfunctorily by politeness as to be actually ruder—could have arisen from shyness, haste, or lack of practice, rather than some personal dislike of Elie (as a Jew, a usurer, Brine's creditor, etc.). Anyway, so long as she was kind to Brine, surely it didn't make much difference how she spoke to Elie, or why.

Yes, he would have to ask Miss Turner about the house. Possibly he would have to get used to a great deal of his correspondence with Brine going through Miss Turner. He didn't *like* the idea, but he could do it. Cheerfully and efficiently, even. Maybe a little too cheerfully, maybe Brine's wife would think him a rattlepate, but what of that? "Do you plan to have children?" Might as well get it all over with now.

"One doesn't *plan* to have children."

Elie took a deep breath. He could do this, too. "Maybe not," he said delicately, "but people have been known to plan *not* to have them."

He heard Brine's slow exhale. "I suppose that will be up to Sarah, too. She'll be the one waking up in the middle of the night if they cry. Don't worry, I'll—ask her that myself. She might be shocked and quote Scripture. Of course I'll pay for them if she wants them." He huffed a frustrated breath. "That sounded unfeeling. I know you don't purchase children at a ship chandlery." The mattress shifted. "Let's talk about anything other than my finances. You must be sick to death of the subject."

"I don't have many other interests," Elie confessed. "Occasionally I read guidebooks and take walks. It's all very thrilling."

"I don't want thrills." The mattress shifted again, some unknown part of Brine actually grazing Elie's thigh. "No—I do want them, and I wish to God I didn't." His voice came from somewhere near Elie's knee. He had lain down, Elie realized.

"It makes me disgusted with myself to think *Perhaps today there'll be a battle* after six months of blockade."

"Isn't that—valor, or something? I thought the Navy encouraged that sort of thing."

Brine's breath stirred Elie's cuff. "Maybe. Sometimes I think I crave unhealthy excitements."

Elie panicked and fell back on an ill-considered joke. "Such as frigging books, you mean." Drat, would Brine even remember his exchange with the boatswain's mate? *He* didn't dwell on every moment he spent with Elie, and a joke you had to explain was never—

Brine burst out laughing. "Oh, that's harmless enough, if you don't gum the pages together."

Elie, having dissipated some of the tension in the bed—in the *room*—said quietly, "So long as you resist temptation, I don't think your private desires can be held against you."

"But is that true?" Brine pressed. "And *have* I resisted temptation? There are degrees of…"

The tension returned in full force. Poor Brine trusted Elie to act in his best interests and give him reasonable advice, and Elie had never trusted himself less or felt less reasonable. "If being bored would make you feel more virtuous, I'd be happy to read you a guidebook," he said lightly. "I think one or two have escaped Lottie's depredations."

"I don't think that would help," Brine said. "You know how books affect me. But perhaps you could advise me which of the attractions of Portsmouth are likely to be open Sunday? Solitary bibliological recreation will have to wait until my spectacles are mended."

"There won't be much open but the taverns, I'm afraid. Don't start any brawls. Kosher steaks aren't cheap, and I'm not wasting one on a black eye."

"What if someone picks a fight with me?"

Elie couldn't think of a joke—couldn't really think of much beyond Brine's voice, warm and soft as astrakhan against Elie's skin. "Have some sense," he said at random.

Brine sighed. "I'll try. Here, you've got to get up early in the morning." He pulled the bedcurtains back. "Thanks for looking in on me, and listening to my nonsense."

"Shall I open your shutters? Or leave the candle?"

His pale eyes were dark in the candlelight, his mouth a shadow. "No, that's all right."

Back in his own room, Elie hesitated, then whistled *Pipe down hammocks*, the boatswain's call for retiring belowdecks at evening. A very clumsy imitation, but maybe Brine hadn't heard it—

Brine whistled back. A much more competent whistle, trilled here and there. Elie didn't recognize the signal. He'd only known *pipe down* by pure chance.

He rested his hand on the wall for a moment, and blew out the candle.

SUNDAY

SECOND DAY OF ROSH HASHANAH

Traditional wardroom toast:
"Absent friends."

Morris was glassy-eyed and inarticulate at breakfast. "The baby..." He sighed. "The baby. I'll fix your glasses tonight after shul. If my hands are steady. Maybe tomorrow morning.

Maybe I can nap under my tallis between shofar blasts."

But he remembered that evening when they arrived home, and asked the maid, Patty, "Where's Mr. Brine? I promised to fix his glasses."

"He's not here, Mr. Morris."

"He went to Mrs. Armstrong's gin-shop," said Lottie irritably. She had minded the littlest children as an excuse to miss the afternoon service, but now she passed Reuben to her grandmother with relief. "He's bound to stumble home any minute to shatter everybody's romantic ideal of him. I put your guidebooks back in your room, Uncle Elie. Except the *Reize in Hongarijen*, I'm reading that."

Morris rolled his eyes. "An inglês and a sailor and you expected him not to drink? The seamen get a half-pint of rum a day, and *they* have to go aloft. Imagine what the officers pour down their gullets."

"He'd have spent the day reading if you'd fixed his glasses," Elie said without much conviction. "Nothing else is open Sunday. That Hungary travelogue's a bit dense, isn't it, Lottie? Your Dutch must be even better than I thought… Beg pardon?"

"I have to read a lot of words aloud before I recognize them," Lottie repeated, raising her voice to be heard over the fussing baby. "But I've got the dictionary you gave me."

Aunt Hava clucked her tongue at her tiny grandson. "You won't go to gin-shops when you're big, will you, meu anjo?"

"It's *probably* Reuben's fault," Lottie grumbled. "The noise would drive anyone to drink. I shall be next."

Elie slipped out amid the resulting hurricane of disapproval. On the one hand, Brine was a grown man, and if he wanted to carouse and drink gin, that was his affair. On the other hand, someone should probably make sure no one was lifting his watch or luring him into dark alleys. Dim alleys, anyway; it wouldn't be *dark* for another hour or so.

Blue coats crowded Mrs. Armstrong's shop, but Elie picked out Brine at once. He was propped up on the end of the counter between two enormous casks, turning an empty penny glass in his hand.

Elie pushed his way over. "Good afternoon."

"Afternoon." Brine executed an about-face, leaning back on his elbows with a grin. "Don't worry, I'm being careful with your money. Only brought what I planned to spend. Didn't buy food. Just gin—economical." Surely he didn't *mean* to glow like that. Not at Elie. Surely he didn't mean to angle his hips towards Elie that way. "I usually like it with bitters, but it's the new year, so I'm drinking genever."

Elie threw up his hands. "Brine, for the love of— I don't begrudge you a bloody sandwich."

Brine shrugged. "I only brought threepence. Didn't mean to be here so long." He frowned. "I shouldn't be this drunk on three. What time is it? I didn't wear my watch. You told me not to brawl, and if someone tried to lift that watch, I'd have to thrash him."

Elie raised his eyebrows across the counter at Molly. The pretty gin-spinner winked and made a complicated gesture that translated quite clearly to *He's had six, but you can pay me later, I know you're good for it.* Elie shuddered. Even if Molly didn't give full measure for money, he doubted he could drink a sixpenn'orth of gin and live.

"If you buy a glass, we can toast absent friends." Brine's smile spread. "Usu—sometimes I think of you at that one. But you're not absent today." He fingered one of Elie's cloth buttons. "Not in your dress uniform, I see. Neither'm I. In case I got in a fight after all."

"And did you?"

Brine tilted his head. "…No," he pronounced at last. "It wasn't a fight."

Elie put his face in his hands. "Do you have any bruises I can't see?"

Brine gave a low laugh. "I don't know."

That *wasn't* an invitation to undress him. Brine would be happy with his wife. He had to be. Elie couldn't stand it if he wasn't. "If it wasn't a fight, what was it?"

"Discipline," Brine enunciated with surprising crispness. "My duty as an officer."

"I see," Elie said skeptically.

"A young fellow was arguing with a Jew in the street. The Jew wanted to buy the boy's watch… Lad said he had a midshipman's berth on the *Vindictive*."

Elie began to have an inkling of what was coming.

"He said his mother in Edinburgh had paid twelve guineas for the watch. That was a whopper, but it did look new. Said he needed money to live on now the *Vindictive*'s launch was delayed, but wouldn't sell to any—" Brine cleared his throat. "I won't repeat it, but he was damned insulting. What's that word that means 'disgrace'?"

"Shonde."

"Yes! A shonde to the service. Then he pointed at me, and said I looked a gentleman and he'd sell to me for six guineas."

Elie groaned.

"The poor Jew seemed resigned to ill treatment. He drew me aside and told me to take the bargain and he'd repay me after, with a guinea over for my trouble."

Molly was smirking behind Brine. Elie glared at her. "You didn't do it, did you?"

"Of course not!" Brine drew himself up as best he could. "I made the lad humbly beg the Jew's pardon and take his money."

Elie burst out laughing, despite all his best intentions. Poor Brine looked utterly nonplussed. "It's a common swindle," Elie explained, not seeing any way out of it now. "You give the boy your money, you never see either of them again, and the watch is worthless. Never buy a watch in the street, *ever*."

Brine took this in.

"But you should be proud! You were true blue. I'm touched by your—"

"Stupidity," Brine finished.

"I didn't spot the trick by being *clever*. I've just heard it before." His lips twitched. "Meanwhile, your purity of heart was a shield and a bulwark—"

Brine gave him a little shove. "Oh, go to hell."

"Why don't I take you home instead?"

Brine resisted. "I can't appear before your female relations drunk."

"Why not?"

"It isn't proper. Disrespectful. What if I curse?"

He decided not to tell Brine that Lottie had already warned them to expect it. "You just don't want to shatter their romantic ideal of you. Don't worry, I'll smuggle you upstairs under cover of dimness. Come along, let's get some food into you."

But when he'd deposited a stumbling Brine on the bed and tried to turn away, Brine didn't loosen his grip on Elie's coat.

Putting his hands on Brine's to pry them off felt unthinkable; so did slipping out of the coat. He tried saying cheerfully, "I'll go and fetch you a sandwich now."

Brine pulled him closer.

6

Elie grimaced at the gin fumes—then nearly overbalanced when Brine let go of him to fall back on the mattress, slinging an arm across his eyes. "I don't know how you make any money when you're so kind."

"I'm not so kind to everybody."

"Is that true?"

Elie's stomach turned over. "I'm not as kind to *you* as you seem to believe."

"If you despised me, would I know it?"

The question startled him. "I can't say. Openly despising clients is very bad for business."

The corner of Brine's mouth turned up. He wasn't tall, yet there was an improbable quantity of him to look at: the veins and tendons in his wrist, wantonly exposed by his worn cuff; the white wool at his knee, pulled into radiating creases by a row of small brass buttons; a reddened patch on the underside of his chin, where he'd shaved too closely; the dark hollow beneath his lower lip.

"Can you keep a secret?" Elie asked.

The mouth twisted. "Yes."

"Promise you won't repeat this."

"On my sacred honor. On my life."

"Ojo!" Elie made a sign against the evil eye. "Sometimes a handshake and a signature is all that's required."

He frowned. "But I don't know yet what you're going to tell me."

Elie could smile as fondly as he liked, since Brine wasn't looking at him. "When I'm out of charity with a client, I sign myself 'your most humble and obedient servant.'"

The frown deepened for a moment, then cleared. Brine broke out in a broad grin. "That's all right, then. You mostly sign mine 'your devoted servant.'"

Elie didn't trust his voice to answer.

Brine laughed. "You've opened Pandora's box now. You'll be getting letters from me like 'What did I do to put you out of countenance on June the second, 1809?'"

"Sandwich," Elie said, and bolted.

Brine's drunkenness had progressed by the time Elie returned with challah and slices of cold tongue. He was curled on his side, face buried in the crook of his elbow. "Don't make me eat. Haven't been this seasick in ages. Damn the North Sea anyway. Only place a ship wallows like this. Next cruise, I want the Mediterranean."

"I'll look out for a vacancy."

"Can we go on deck? Fresh air…"

Elie opened the window as wide as it would go. "The sky's red."

"Sailor's delight." Brine breathed in deeply. "How's the barometer?"

"Steady."

"Wind?"

Elie stuck his hand out the window. "In the southwest."

"Good."

"Have some bread, it's soft."

Brine nibbled plaintively.

"And some barley-water."

Without opening his eyes, Brine heaved himself upright and put out his hand. Elie put the tankard in it. "It might come up again," Brine warned. "Where's the basin?"

Elie took it off the dressing table and slid it under the bed within easy reach.

"If I'm sick, will that…? Maybe you should go."

Elie's heart swelled. "It won't shatter my romantic ideal of you. I swear on my sacred honor." Brine poked him. Elie jumped, letting out an unfortunate squeak.

Brine bit the corner of his mouth. "Are you ticklish, Mr. Eleazar?"

"No. Careful, the tankard's got a lid."

He opened one eye to get his bearings. "This is prettier than the one you sold me," he said accusingly.

"No it isn't."

He gulped down half the barley-water and came up gasping, wiping his mouth with the back of his hand. "There's a little man smoking a pipe on it. Mine's just pewter."

"You live on a ship. I don't sell you breakable things unless there's no way around it."

"Like my watch," Brine said affectionately. He took another long draught, licking the corner of his mouth.

Elie went up like dry powder. "Sorry, what was that?"

Brine set the tankard aside and curled up again. "I've changed my mind. Read me a guidebook."

"Really?"

"Please. The trick to being seasick is not to think about it. But it's very hard not…"

"Not to think about it?"

"Mm."

So Elie carried in a lamp and an armful of books. "I'd better eat before the fast starts at sunset. Did you want any more bread?" Brine shook his head, so Elie made himself a sandwich and sat on the floor, spreading out his books (which mostly lacked covers) face-up to show the title pages. "So," he said between bites, "we've got *A Companion and Useful Guide to the Beauties of Scotland and the Hebrides*—I haven't read that one yet, but Lottie liked it; *Geological Travels in Some Parts of France, Switzerland, and Germany*; *Guide to All the Watering and Sea-Bathing Places in England and Wales*; *Lex Mercatoria or A Complete Code of Commercial Law*—"

"The *Lex Mercatoria*'s not a guidebook."

"Oh, no? What about the accounts of the commerce of other nations with their weights and measures, then?"

From this angle, Brine's arm hid his mouth. When a sliver of smile peeped out, Elie had an impulse to say the prayer for the first sight of a new moon.

"Then, um, Russia and Sweden—oh, but that one's in Portuguese. I'd better stick to English, hadn't I?"

"I'd take it as a mercy."

"That leaves Ireland; Buenos Aires to Lima; *The New Seaman's Guide and Coaster's Companion*—"

"That one," Brine said firmly.

Elie laughed at him. "Really?"

"Yes."

He opened the book at random. "To the westward of Folkstone, a ledge of rocks stretches off to a full mile from shore, having 12 fathoms close-to. Stand therefore no nearer to the shore than 13 or 14 fathoms; nor farther off than 18 fathoms. You may anchor in Romney Bay, with a westerly wind, in 8, 10, or 12 fathoms, with Dungeness bearing SW by W or WSW…"

Brine made a contented sound. Elie's heart turned over. He didn't dare look up. Brine would hear his voice change, if he did.

MONDAY
FAST OF GEDALIAH

Traditional wardroom toast:
"Our ships at sea."

Morris squinted through the unbroken left lens of Brine's glasses. "The same strength again?"

"I think so." Brine turned to keep the sun out of his eyes, looking wan and wilted.

Morris pushed two pairs of spectacles across the counter. "Try these and tell me if they're better."

Brine obeyed. "No, thank you." He pressed his fingers to his temple.

Morris set his thumbs on the broken lens and popped it out of the frame, then selected a fresh lens from a shallow, velvet-lined drawer beneath the counter. "Try this pair." He pointed with his elbow. "They fold in half to fit in your waistcoat pocket."

"Do you mind if I look at the books?" Elie asked. Otherwise, he'd end up absentmindedly staring at Brine.

"Not in the least," Morris said. "We've nothing to be ashamed of, now Lottie keeps them."

So Elie ran his eyes soothingly over orders and client

accounts, listening with half an ear as Morris pointed out blue spectacles for reading in artificial light, a green pair to lessen glare on water, pairs with broad, flat rims of tortoiseshell or horn to prevent excess light wearying the eye…

Lottie's books were really getting very good. Scarcely an obvious arithmetic error in sight, and she'd obviously been applying herself since appropriating Elie's dogeared copy of *The Young Clerk's Assistant; Or, Penmanship Made Easy, Instructive and Entertaining* last summer. His cousins' occasional hasty entries were easy to spot among her small, precise script and well-formed numerals. When she rushed, though, she still made those darling little *B*s with the fat lower bow almost swallowing the upper.

Smiling, Elie slid the ledger towards Brine to show it off, and noticed his client looking rather dizzy. "Don't buy anything unless you really want it," he said pointedly.

"Don't make me out to be a bully," Morris said. "I think you'll find I'm doing your client a favor."

"From the goodness of your heart," Elie said, still more pointedly. "He doesn't owe you a return."

"I never said he did," Morris snapped. Ah, the age-old tradition of bickering on fast days. "It was probably my baby that woke him in the middle of the night and made him step on his glasses in the first place."

Brine gulped and picked up the green spectacles. But his brow smoothed out when he put them on; tentatively, he turned to let the sun fall on his face.

"Only a crown and a half," Morris said mildly.

Elie pointed at the ledger. "Lottie's handwriting is getting better than mine, don't you think?" As soon as Brine bent his head to look, Elie gave his cousin a significant glance over the top of it.

"Oh, very nice!" Brine said. "But she's young. Your own everyday script was more painstaking at eighteen."

Morris looked confused. Elie stared harder.

"Ah." Morris pushed Brine's mended glasses across the counter, smooth and shining like new. "Why don't you take that green pair on trial? If you want them when your leave ends, what would you say to writing a testimonial to their usefulness?"

"Certainly," Brine said.

"If you give me leave to print it above your name, we'll call that payment in full."

Thank you, Elie mouthed.

"I couldn't accept," Brine protested. "I've got prize money coming."

Morris waved this away. "Ah, you wouldn't believe the price of advertising these days. If anyone admires the glasses, you might just direct them to me. Here, some of my trade cards have a nautical design."

Elie nudged the stack of cards back towards his cousin just as Brine laughed and picked it up, their fingers brushing. "I've no objection." He gave Elie a mischievous glance. "Well. I object to both officers in this engraving wearing epaulets."

"I have to communicate my elegance and exclusivity somehow," Morris said dryly. He threaded black ribbon through the loops in each earpiece, and handed the green glasses over.

Brine took them with thanks and a handshake, before turning to Elie. "Will we pass the sea-wall— That is, what business have you got today, Mr. Eleazar?"

"I've got some errands for other clients." Elie shifted guiltily. "I'll work on the *Vliegende Draeck* accounting as soon as I'm finished."

"Would I be in the way?"

Elie blinked. "On my errands? It's more likely you'd be *bored* on my errands."

Brine fussed with deciding where to tie off the ribbon on his new glasses. "Will any of them take you along the sea-wall? I want to see how these do with the glare."

"You could sit and read on the sea-wall all day if you liked," Elie pointed out. "You're on leave."

Brine slipped the glasses on with a shrug. "Your talk of handwriting reminded me it's almost time to copy my logbook to send to London."

"But I usually do that for you."

"Well—you seem a bit swamped, honestly, and you haven't got any mates. Junior clerks, I mean. I thought I'd spare you the trouble. My handwriting isn't too abominable, is it?"

Morris rolled his eyes. "Elie would be glad of your company. He just isn't sure whether it's good English manners to say so. Run along now, I have lenses to grind."

Brine's grin broke out. Elie hoped the green glass would mask his blush.

Somehow the short walk from Queen Street to the Point took upwards of two hours. Some of the delays were necessary: buying Elie's new calendar, visiting various pawnshops and ship chandleries for his clients, purchasing

Brine's luncheon. Others emphatically were not, such as climbing the church tower and listening to Brine's detailed appraisal first of the green spectacles, then of the rigging of every ship within range of his pocket spyglass.

"Our ships at sea," he toasted with his flask of peppermint-water, looking haler already. He caught Elie watching him drink. "Does it bother you? I can put it away. Low rations aren't so bad, until you smell food."

Elie shook his head. "It's only for one day. The trick is not to think about it, like you said last night."

"Sometimes it's easier than others." Brine leaned out over the railing, drawn irresistibly towards the horizon. His hair blew about his face. "What else don't you think about, Mr. Eleazar?"

The fast of Gedaliah was only one day—was one of only three fasts all year that he kept. Yet it felt familiar. It felt as though Elie spent his whole life pretending not to mind the hunger gnawing at him from the inside out, while other people ate their fill. "I don't know," he lied easily, familiarly. "If I did, then I'd be thinking about it, wouldn't I?"

In the counting-house, Brine borrowed a lap-desk and sprawled cheerfully on the floor by the window, slipping on his refurbished reading glasses with a contented sound. Elie, finally sifting through the last of his correspondence, unearthed several matters requiring his urgent attention—a week ago, for preference, but certainly before he could begin on the *Vliegende Draeck* file.

He hesitated over Brine's letter, the seal still unbroken. His reluctance to read it in its author's presence was absurd, but in good conscience he should attend to drearier obligations first, anyway...

"Can you spare a moment to check this tally?" Brine fisted a hand in his hair. "I know the figures are right, but I can't make it square."

Elie pushed back his chair, tucking the letter into his new calendar.

TUESDAY
Traditional wardroom toast:
"Our men."

"I don't mind the North Sea so much when I'm *in* it," Brine said languorously. His head rested against the lip of the steaming pool, his profile a minor miracle: closed eyelid and damp lashes; bead of water suspended at the tip of his nose; forceful jaw; Adam's apple and long arc of throat, water pooling in his exposed clavicle. His skin was rosy and damp, his lips red.

Bathing clothes were made of brown canvas, on the theory that it was neither transparent nor clinging. This was true, but only relative to other fabrics.

You should be working on his prize accounting right now. The least you can do is not ogle him. Solomon had probably had a proverb about that. Elie should have paid more attention to his Hebrew tutor.

Then Elie remembered that he *had* paid attention to his

Hebrew tutor. Mostly the kind he was paying Brine now. "The slothful man says, 'There's a lion outside, I'll be killed in the street.'"

Brine's lashes fluttered. "What?"

Elie dropped his gaze. "I recalled an apt proverb. On the subject of justifying procrastination."

Brine's hand emerged from the water with a ripple and settled on Elie's right shoulder. No—on the muscle between shoulder and neck, which constant writing had made sore for so long he'd stopped noticing it.

Looking at Brine must have kept Elie from thinking about his other senses. All at once, he was aware of heated seawater and rough canvas against his skin. He smelled sweat and salt. He heard the clamor and echo of voices and footsteps, boilers and pumps and the nearby surf. He noticed his mouth watering.

The ball of Brine's thumb dug into his flesh and rolled upwards. Elie understood afresh the daily prayer he'd stopped noticing, too: *You formed man in wisdom, and created inside him many openings and hollow places.* With shocking immediacy, he felt the hydraulics in his own heart. His fingers and toes prickled as life rushed in.

If Elie wasn't careful, life and blood would be pumped into another neglected extremity of his body—presently obscured by brown canvas and a couple of feet of seawater, but he'd have to stand up sometime.

Brine's hand fell to the tile. Elie hoped it was the salt and sweat that made his eyes sting. Half his neck felt disconcertingly relaxed. He raised his own slack hand to massage the other side. "I don't mind the North Sea so much when I'm in it, either."

Brine gave him a perplexed look.

"Sorry. I meant it's warm here and I don't want to go back to work."

"Everything has an end—and a pudding has two." Brine laughed. "Solomon must wish he'd thought of that one." His laughter sounded different today. Lighter, richer, more immediately physical.

Maybe it was only the echo in the long, tiled room, but Elie suspected the difference was in his own ears. This sound had been air filling Brine's lungs, had slid up his throat and tangled at the back of his mouth. If he looked at Brine, he'd see amusement tightening his belly, stretching his mouth wide, kissing the corners of his eyes.

He didn't look.

"Don't think about work in leisure hours," Brine went on. "It spoils the leisure and accomplishes no work. You'll be at the counting-house in an hour. Until then, be here…" His voice dropped, the last words unintelligible in the din. *With me?* Maybe if Elie had been looking, he'd have caught them.

Brine's advice was quite apt for what Elie had pretended he was talking about, but useless for what he'd actually been talking about. Love wasn't a gin-shop; Elie couldn't turn a valve and dispense precisely a penny's worth of blood to his heart, or his cock, and then go about his business.

Or—maybe that was what he did alone in his bed at night. Maybe tonight, in the dark, he'd shut his eyes and turn the valve. Maybe then he could let himself *be here* with Brine, just for a few minutes. But now? Now Elie had no choice but to not think about it.

So he did. He stopped noticing the water on his skin, the

salt in the air, Brine's beautiful body crafted by the Almighty in loving kindness. "I have to work on the *Draeck* accounting," he said. "Sorry. Stay as long as you like."

"I'll come with you," Brine said readily. "I was here for ages on Saturday, anyway."

Elie gritted his teeth and trudged back to the dressing room, chatting with Brine while they stripped and toweled off. He concentrated on dressing without dragging his tzitzit on the muddy floor, instead of on Brine, rubbing himself dry with enough energy to set his cock bobbing, or on any of the other cocks scattered about the crowded room.

"Slow down, Mr. Eleazar. You'll take a chill if you leave a hot room for the cold street still damp."

"It's only September, and we're not actually in the North Sea—"

"Are you truly just conscientious?" Brine straightened, towel dangling in one hand like he was posing for a statue. "Or is something else afoot?"

All at once, Elie was cold and shaky, his mouth as dry as if a valve *had* been turned, somewhere. He swallowed twice before he could get out, "Something else? Like what?"

"I *can* amuse myself if I'm in your way," Brine said. "I promise not to go back to the gin-shop, if that's what's worrying you. Or if I've—offended you in some way, tell me so I can apologize."

"Brine! You haven't done anything. I simply have a lot of work to do." Elie never liked lingering in the dressing room anyway—but if he told Brine about the time a stranger had offered him a penny for a good look at a circumcised cock, Brine would be so distressed, and it would be turning honesty into a lie, a calculated cover for Elie's excessive interest in Brine's own cock. "And I'm a bit shy," he settled on. "The public baths aren't really my…"

"And you're sure that's all?"

Elie nodded.

Brine relaxed, spreading his towel over a bench to lay out his clothes. "Why are the prettiest fellows always the shyest?" He laughed. "I suppose I've answered my own question: they're sick of being looked at. I'm glad you're not cross with me, anyway." He dug in his pockets for a crumpled square of muslin, from which he extracted a sadly reduced bar of salve and began rubbing it into his damp skin. "Would you do my back? I can ask somebody else, if you're too shy."

Elie was so distracted by about five different things that had just happened, that saying no seemed to require more effort than taking the salve. "I don't remember selling you this," he rambled, so as to not think about Brine's back yielding under the pressure of his fingers. "Not that I expect a monopoly. But I hope it wasn't that wretched Bulldog…"

"Who?"

"Another trader—on the Hard, with a wooden bulldog over his door. He got his start as a barker. He probably *is* a better salesman than most, but he's such a braggart about it, and oh, does he love a monopoly. He's started selling bars of salve with a clever name…what is it?"

"You mean 'All Hands On Deck'!" said a nearby sailor. "Great stuff. They sell it on the Hard at the sign of the bulldog. You can use it everywhere, not just hands."

Another nearby man guffawed. "I've heard men swear by it for buggery."

General hilarity.

Elie had been wondering where precisely Brine expected him to put his hands. With a shock of clarity, he realized: only where Brine couldn't reach himself. Elie's hands were already much too low. He gave back the salve, and sat to wait for Brine's glorious mop of hair to dry.

Brine was laughing too. "I appreciate the testimonial, sir, but my sweetheart makes this for me. I'm sure she'll bring another bar when I see her this evening."

"When you—" Elie's voice cracked. "*What?*"

7

Brine glanced at him. "When I see her this evening." His eyes widened. "Is there some difficulty? You didn't say anything, so I thought it must be all right."

"Miss Turner is coming *here*? Today?"

"I must have mentioned that," Brine said. "I know I told you all about it in my letter—shit, I forgot you hadn't got it! But didn't I see you with it yesterday at the counting-house— No, of course it's my fault." He looked stricken.

Elie wanted to reassure him, but *not thinking about it* had somehow ballooned into not thinking at all. His mind was empty.

"And she already thinks I'm useless," Brine said bitterly. "She's tactful about it—you're all so bloody tactful about it, and I'm so bloody useless ashore." He scrubbed at his hair with the towel. "She's a bride, for Christ's sake. She's coming to marry me, and I can't even…"

She's coming to marry me. Of course she was. It might be years before Brine next had leave.

"I'll take care of it," Elie said numbly. He took his calendar from his pocket, and slid out Brine's letter. The damp heat had softened the seal; a fingernail quickly did the rest.

…Your aunt's impeccable hospitality…your kindness…my betrothed…Tuesday evening… When he brought the letter close to his face to make out a smudged word, he smelled

cardamom and orange peel, the traces of Brine's salve on his hands. His hunger felt blessedly distant. "Which coach is she arriving on, do you know?"

"All she wrote was Tuesday evening. I'm so sorry. I'll pay you extra, or if you give me very clear instructions— Maybe one of the children could help me arrange things—"

"Does that mean she's leaving Birmingham on Tuesday evening, that she's catching the London-to-Portsmouth coach on Tuesday evening, or that she's arriving here Tuesday evening?"

"I thought…arriving. But she didn't say. I'm sure she didn't."

Elie squared his shoulders. "All right," he said cheerfully. "I'll sort it out."

"How?"

Since coaches dropped passengers all over Portsmouth, the only way to sort it out was by tipping people all over Portsmouth to watch for her and send a message to Aunt Hava's, then tipping the messenger. "Oh, I know people," he said vaguely. "Have you her portrait, by any chance?"

Brine's face brightened. "I can draw one."

"Splendid." Elie returned to the letter. *I've been given to understand that marriage by license requires a month's residence, but can that be got round?* In Elie's experience, most things could be got round if someone was willing to perjure himself. But where *did* one get an Anglican marriage license in Portsmouth? "Do you know what archdeaconry we're in?"

Brine shook his head. Elie would have to inquire at the church. Shit, what if they had to travel up to the bishop's offices in Winchester? He'd never finish the blasted prize accounting at this rate.

No, someone in Portsmouth *must* be able to grant marriage licenses. Brine was hardly the first sailor to marry in a port town. But Heaven knew what the fees would be. And in London, Elie knew which Doctors' Commons clerks were sticklers for the letter of the law, and which were lax. Who might be able to tell him that here?

He scribbled some notes… Mrs. Lopez had a room to let, and she might be amenable to saying Miss Turner had been with her a month. Unless she'd already found another lodger. He'd better go straight there, and he'd have to pay for tonight whether or not Miss Turner actually arrived—

"Mr. Eleazar."

Elie jumped.

"Sorry. Didn't mean to startle you." Brine was fully dressed, hat under his arm. His hair—though damp at the roots—had dried enough for the short walk to the counting-house. And he looked subdued, biting the inside of his lip in a way that made it pout a little.

Elie glanced at his watch and realized he'd ignored Brine for a quarter of an hour. "Sorry," he said with a self-deprecating little laugh—his professional laugh. He hadn't used it with Brine in a few days.

A deeper shadow passed over Brine's face.

Elie should probably have felt guilty. Instead he thought sharply, *How did you fail to mention your betrothed's imminent arrival for three whole days?* Because Brine hadn't mentioned it. Elie would have remembered. Surely a man who was looking forward to his bride's arrival would have talked of nothing else.

Unless Elie hadn't hidden his dislike of the subject as well as he'd thought. He felt queasy. "I wasn't supposed to send her a ticket, was I?"

Brine grimaced. "She didn't say anything about it. Are they very expensive?"

So now Elie had to *hope* for Miss Turner's arrival…at some unspecified point in the next two days. Actually, he had to hope for her arrival *today*. Tomorrow was the Michaelmas quarter day, and most of it would be taken up with queuing at the Navy Pay Office.

"Mr. Eleazar?"

"Sorry." Elie laughed self-deprecatingly again. "Thanks for a very pleasant morning, but it's back to business for me, I'm afraid."

"Can't I help? At least I could keep you company."

Elie tried to frame a diplomatic refusal. It wasn't Brine's fault that his presence hampered Elie's ability to do simple sums, let alone balance a precarious mental clockwork of tasks and times. Nor was it his fault that Elie planned to cover all the extra costs he was about to incur on Miss Turner's behalf. With perfect propriety, for once—since it was *also* not Brine's fault that Elie hadn't read his letter—but Brine would be sure to object anyway. "I'll be dull company."

"Don't be—"

"Forgive me. I just—have a lot to do today, and it's more efficient if I do it the way I'm used to, on my own. But that likeness of Miss Turner would be a great help. And can you keep Aunt Hava apprised of your whereabouts? I'll send word as soon as I find out where to apply for a marriage license."

Brine's smile was very nearly convincing; only a few deep crow's feet at the corners of his eyes gave him away. "Of course. Thank you."

Why didn't the silence on the way to the counting-house make it any easier to think?

Once there, Elie took his lists of tasks—Brine and Miss Turner's tasks, quarter-day tasks, *Vliegende Draeck* tasks—and divided them up by location. Even that, he couldn't manage without frequent glances at Brine's absorbed expression, at his self-assured pencil-strokes, at the deft, precise swipe of eraser and thumb for light and shade.

At last Brine blew on his paper and laid it on Elie's blotter.

Elie had actually known rather a lot about Miss Turner already. For example:

(1) The color of her hair. (Not quite dark enough to look black by candlelight.) Brine kept a lock of it in his bow-compass case.

(2) Her measurements. (Five foot five, small bosom, slight.) Elie had helped arrange for a secondhand mourning wardrobe when her brother had died a few years ago.

(2) Her handwriting. (A workaday Sunday-school copperplate, well suited to her brusque prose.)

So really, the portrait shouldn't have surprised him. Brine had drawn an elegant oval face, very English—skeptical brows above clear eyes and long straight nose, mouth tucked in at the corners, sharp chin—and hinted at narrow shoulders and bust. She looked as if she was in a hurry, but had paused a moment to humor the artist. Her adornment was as perfunctory as her writing, the ringlets at her temples crooked and too numerous, as though she'd been thinking of something else and overshot her mark.

But Elie *was* surprised by his pang at the suppressed amusement in that tucked-in mouth, the gleam in her eyes and the faint lines Brine had sketched under them, tired and human. *It doesn't matter whether she likes me,* he'd told himself for years. And the drawing made him wish she would.

But maybe it was only that he saw her through Brine's eyes. Brine did love her. That much was obvious.

"Is this the *Cocksure*'s Prize List?" Brine pulled the sheaf of paper towards him, and ran his finger regretfully down the wardroom names at the top. "Look how many of us are dead already. Poor Quibell—'deceased June 1813, no family.' He'd have been married in another month, but now the girl won't see a penny of his twelve hundred pounds. That gave me a kick in the arse, all right. We had to take up a collection for her to buy mourning clothes." He tossed the list back onto the file. "What was that proverb about justifying procrastination?"

"The slothful man says, 'There's a lion outside, I'll be killed in the street.'" There was an awkward pause.

Brine roused himself. "Will the drawing do? It's been a few years since I saw her, but I think it's a decent likeness." He frowned. "She may have changed her hair. And I don't think the upper lip is quite right…"

"She's very pretty," Elie said. "Here's tracing paper, can you make seven copies?"

Elie gave the portraits to the porter's oldest daughter, along with seven pennies and instructions to find someone she trusted to watch for Miss Turner everywhere the coaches dropped passengers.

If Lottie could be spared from the shop to inquire about the license and Miss Turner's berth at the boardinghouse, he could start in on the prize accounting as soon as he'd gone over his tally of monies to be collected at the Pay Office tomorrow.

They were delicate inquiries, though, full of conditions

and contingencies. If Lottie failed to clarify some particular regarding the license, Elie might have to go back himself anyway, and everyone's time would have been wasted.

He stared down at the Prize List, lying haphazardly atop a small mountain of *Vliegende Draeck* papers in English, Dutch, and German, with some Danish thrown in just to be contrary. His eyes were drawn irresistibly to two words: *Augustus Brine.*

What if you told them there's no way around the residency requirement? an insidious voice suggested.

Horrified at himself, Elie put on his coat and set out for the church.

He was emphatically snubbed by several vicars and curates. Evidently, a couple, married by license in Portsmouth Church several years ago, were now embroiled in protracted and acrimonious legal proceedings over the validity of said license, and the Portsmouth clergy were determined not to be embarrassed again.

Elie decided to try the dockyard chaplain. Having stopped at Mrs. Lopez's boardinghouse on his way, he was walking along the Hard when he saw a slight, dark-haired, tight-lipped woman striding out of the Bulldog's shop.

Probably it was another oval-faced English brunette. Brine had said Tuesday evening, and it was barely Tuesday afternoon.

But she hurried along, set to pass him with mere inches of pavement between them, and Elie's professional instincts triumphed. "Miss Turner of Birmingham?"

She stiffened, dodging towards the nearest shop window, and narrowed her eyes at him. "Do I know you, sir?"

"Only if you're Sarah Turner, and only by

correspondence." He bowed. "I'm Eleazar Benezet, agent to Augustus Brine of the *Steadfast*."

Her expression relaxed into mere wary suspicion. "How did you recognize me?"

Elie slid Brine's drawing out of his pocket calendar and handed it to her with one of his own cards.

Drat, there they were—the bright eyes and fond, tamped-down smile. "Augie flattered me."

"Not really."

The skeptical eyebrows went up. "I didn't expect him to be looking for me yet; I caught an earlier coach."

"How was your journey?" Elie asked, to avoid the whole subject.

"Dusty and jouncing, obviously."

"I hope you caught fleeting glimpses of many fine houses and churches?"

She frowned.

Elie trotted out the self-deprecating laugh. "I've arranged lodging for you at a very respectable house. May I escort you? I can send someone for your luggage."

"I hope you will not take it amiss," she said blandly, "if I do not blithely follow at your heels. After all, you *could* have waylaid Mr. Brine and picked his pockets."

"Very sensible," Elie said with equal blandness. "Would you like to wait here while I fetch him?"

She tapped her chin, considering. "No, thank you. Pray ask him to meet me at King James's Gate at four."

His blandness failed him. "He hasn't seen you in years!"

She looked self-conscious, then annoyed. "I have some errands to run. After so many years, two more hours won't kill him."

"I would be happy to take charge of any commissions—"

"Thank you, no. I should prefer to arrange for my own lodging, as well. I hope you didn't pay anything down."

Elie wavered.

"How much? I suppose I can defray part—"

"It's not that." Elie would much rather have let Brine explain all this, but in another two hours *she* might have paid for a room in advance. "I understand you've come to marry Mr. Brine?"

She hesitated. Surely *that* wasn't a prying question. "Ye-es."

"He won't be in port long enough for banns. A license requires a month's residence in the parish where it's issued."

She bit her cheek. "Does it? I'm afraid I've never been married before."

Elie lowered his voice. "Once the marriage is performed, its legality can't be questioned on grounds of residence. That's guaranteed by statute. But if doubts are raised beforehand, you'll need the boardinghouse mistress to swear you were with her a month."

"That's rather easily disproven, isn't it?"

"No one will care to disprove it. You're both of age and no large fortunes are involved. This is only a precaution."

"Then I don't see why I mayn't choose my own lodging."

Wonderful, go right ahead. "The best-laid schemes of mice and men, et cetera," Elie said. "Better safe than sorry. An ounce of prevention—"

"And what does this boardinghouse of yours cost?" The frown returned in force at his answer. "That's very dear."

"Not for Portsmouth in wartime, I'm afraid. But you needn't trouble yourself about that. Mr. Brine intends to foot the bill."

Her eyes flashed. "He most certainly does not!"

Elie bit his tongue. "I'll let you discuss that with him."

"I shall," she said sharply. "What else does Mr. Brine foot the bill for, pray?"

Elie suddenly realized that Miss Turner suspected him of gouging Brine.

"Are you well, Mr. Benezet?"

"Must have swallowed a fly," he got out. "Nothing to worry about." He took a few deep breaths, until he could say with a straight face, "I'm glad you're looking out for him."

She met his eyes, unblinking. "Somebody has to."

Elie smiled, bland as English cooking again. "It was a pleasure to make your acquaintance at last, Miss Turner. I'll send Mr. Brine word that you've arrived safely and will meet him at King James's Gate at four."

"Mr. Eleazar." She hesitated, then peeled off her dusty right glove and began to put out her hand. Elie was already bowing over it when he saw she'd meant him to shake it. No help for it now. He just hoped she wasn't one of those people who measured a bow with a tangent-screw and expected its altitude to mean something.

"Good day," she said, and strode briskly off before he was fully upright. Well. There it was. Brine's future wife was unmistakably, inescapably corporeal, and she didn't like Elie.

But why *should* Miss Turner like him, when for years he'd resented and ignored her, and built sun-drenched castles in the air at her expense?

Somebody has to look out for him. A knot climbed in his throat—not laughter this time. *He* looked out for Brine. He'd been doing it for years.

Miss Turner had probably known Brine for twenty years before Elie ever laid eyes on him.

Of course Elie knew he wasn't really indispensable to anybody but his mother. So why did realizing he was more dispensable than he'd imagined hurt so much every time?

Shit, he was about to start crying in the middle of the street.

But even that was self-indulgent exaggeration. A minute later, his ticklish throat and aching eyes had lessened. By the time he reached the dockyard, all that was left was a renewed tightness in his shoulders, where Brine had massaged it away just this morning.

8

I t was half three when Elie finished his interview with the dockyard chaplain, plenty of time to traverse King James's Gate and be safely ensconced at the counting-house long before the touching reunion. He strode swiftly back along the Hard—down High Street—but as he passed through the arch onto the Point, he heard pounding footsteps and a glad cry in a familiar voice: "Sarah!"

Instinctively, Elie kept his gaze straight ahead. He kept pace with the crowd. Only when he'd passed the Round Tower did he turn and look.

Brine and Miss Turner were still embracing tightly. They separated at last with every appearance of reluctance, both grinning ear to ear. Yes, even at this distance, Elie could see dour Miss Turner glowing up at Brine like—like a bride. She gave Brine another quick squeeze, looked up into his face, and with a brisk shrug, planted a kiss squarely on his mouth.

Elie turned away, pulling out his watch. Only 3:42. They had both of them been impatient, then. Eager to see each other. Somehow, Elie had let himself forget that how a man *talked* about his wife rarely had anything to do with how he actually felt about her.

He worked through dinner. Not because he didn't want to see Brine. Not because he didn't want to watch Brine raise his glass and toast *Our men!* with a warm glance at Elie that didn't, couldn't, shouldn't mean anything. His quarter-day preparations took him until nine o'clock, that was all. Despite the Pay Office's own recurring scandals over internal graft and embezzlement, they were remarkably quick to cluck their tongues if Elie transposed digits or mistook a nought for a six, and to make reproving murmurs full of words like "irregularities," "abuse of trust," and "withdraw your license."

But at last he stitched the final promotion ticket to its corresponding power of attorney and slid it into his portfolio in alphabetical order. He rubbed his bleary eyes, trying not to think about Morris's reproving murmurs—kinder than the Pay Office's, but full of equally terrifying words such as "vellicate the eye," "decay," and "gradual weakening." He wasn't losing his sight. It was just dark.

Yes, replied his mental simulacrum of Morris, *but if you must work so late, at least use the green lampshade I gave you.*

Elie buried his head in his folded arms to block out the injurious light, and spent five minutes trying to believe that anything good would ever happen to him again.

But what little optimism he'd managed to work up drained away as soon as he stepped from the Lazarus shop into the passageway, and heard Brine and Miss Turner arguing in the kitchen. He eased the door shut, planning to creep up the stairs—

"Mr. Eleazar? Is that you?"

"No," Elie said under his breath, and went into the kitchen, pasting a cheerful expression on his face. "Good evening, Mr. Brine, Miss Turner." They sat side by side in the chairs closest to the fire, the teapot between them. Elie lifted the lid. "Is that a first or second steeping? I could add some fresh leaves." He swung the kettle closer to the fire.

"Thank you, sir," Miss Turner said in steely tones. "But I was just taking my leave. Please convey my compliments to your aunt."

"Of course, ma'am." Elie pulled out her chair for her, hiding his relief.

But Brine, rising as she did, said through his teeth, "Talk some sense into her, Mr. Eleazar. She says she won't marry me until I have the prize money in hand." Elie went cold. "Tell her the money's as good as distributed. God knows when I'll be in England again. God grant I may *ever* be in England again!"

"There's no need to involve Mr. Eleazar in our private affairs, Augie. You've been telling me that money is as good as yours for five years now."

"Closer to four, I think," Elie said. "I do understand your concern, ma'am, but…" He tried never to give assurances about matters not entirely within his control. *Could* he promise no fresh delay, no reversal?

He'd been avoiding the *Vliegende Draeck* accounting to put off Brine's wedding. He had never meant to succeed so totally.

Brine's beautiful mouth was set like flint, his sure fingers tapping their agitation on the back of his chair. Elie had to make this right somehow. "There can be no further legal challenge. The rest is bookkeeping. Perhaps if you describe your concerns, I can allay them." He took a deep breath. "If a further advance for wedding expenses—"

"Thank you, sir, but I fail to see how yet another loan at interest would benefit our household finances. You may not be aware that I shall lose my father's pension upon my marriage."

"Quite aware," said Elie. "But as his wife, Mr. Brine can allot you half his pay. The amount is not *much* less and can be collected more frequently. Indeed, as his wife you will have a great many rights you lack at present."

"Please, Sarah. Let me take care of you." Brine's voice was tight, the Brummie in it stronger after a day with Miss Turner.

Elie spoke differently at home too, quite unconsciously. People talked of polishing an accent, as though you could holystone the rough patches and be left with something smooth and clean. But it was more like adding a copper bottom: the old shape remained, underneath. How else to explain the way years of travel could fade in an afternoon, Elie's mouth settling comfortably into its natural position? Jael's finishing-school diction had scraped off like barnacles after a few days with him, London and Portuguese inflections shining through.

Miss Turner was where Brine was from, where he would always settle comfortably in spite of himself. She was his family.

Elie felt sulky, and hated it. He was a *clerk*. When he was with a client, he was accustomed to feeling brisk and impersonal in an encouraging sort of way, rather like a freshly trimmed pen or a new pocket calendar.

If being a pocket calendar was where you settled comfortably in spite of yourself, why fight destiny? Why not be comfortable, at least?

He took a deep breath, feeling his brow smooth out. He didn't think about it. "Of course it's awkward to bring up," he said, brisk and impersonally encouraging, "but if you're afraid of delay in the prize distribution, that's all the more reason to marry." *Don't think about it.* "An officer's widow is entitled to collect his prize money, which would otherwise revert to Greenwich Hospital." *Don't think about it.* "You will also only be entitled to an eventual naval pension if you marry Mr. Brine while he is on full pay. I've seen many sad cases where an injury deprived a wife of—"

"I am not a *vulture*." Miss Turner's voice shook. "Merely because I'm cautious— How dare you talk about Augie as if he were—an *investment* to me? I'm not— How dare you? He's a human being! He's right there listening to you."

Even if Elie had been able to think of anything impersonal or encouraging to say to that, he couldn't have said it in an impersonal tone. *She'd* brought the money into it, not Elie.

And yet it was Elie who'd have to execute Brine's will, apply for her widow's pension, commission mourning rings from Brine's beautiful hair and distribute them to his family and friends. He would have to pretend Brine had been nothing to him but an investment, while Miss Turner grieved at home in peace and quiet and people told her how sorry they were, and how very brave she was.

He heard the kettle start to vibrate behind them, and affected not to notice. Spilling hot water on his feet would hardly improve matters.

Did Brine believe Elie thought of him as an investment?

But if he did—well, wasn't that what Elie had been striving for all along? To keep Brine from ever knowing just how great a loss Elie was willing to take on him?

He kept his eyes on the table. "I am aware that Mr. Brine is a human being. My apologies if I implied otherwise." Had that sounded impersonal? Elie didn't feel like a person, which must be a good sign.

Brine took the kettle off and refilled the teapot.

"I didn't mean to be harsh…" Miss Turner began.

"It's quite all right," Elie said.

"Don't make me kick *you* in the ankle too," Brine told him. "Of course it's not all right." He poured a cup of tea. For a while, the only sound was his spoon as he dissolved a lump of sugar.

Elie should probably excuse himself. But his feet felt planted to the floor, his hands glued to the back of Miss Turner's empty chair. He couldn't look away from Brine's circling teaspoon. He remembered Brine's hand on his shoulder, kneading.

Brine added cream to his tea, then grated nutmeg over it. Elie could smell it.

He hadn't eaten anything since noon, had he? If there was any apple cake left in the pantry, he'd take a slice upstairs with him. That would settle him. He pried one hand off the chair.

Brine picked up his teacup and held it out, squarely in the center of Elie's field of view.

Elie blinked. The tea waved back and forth slightly. "Um. For…me…?"

The tea hovered patiently. "Yes."

Elie pried his other hand off the chair and took it. The tea was much too sweet, and Elie liked it. When he'd drunk half the cup, he fetched out the apple cake and cut himself a slice, pushing the rest inquiringly towards Miss Turner.

"No, thank you," she said. "I really ought to be going."

"Sarah, may I speak with you in—" Brine glanced around, a bit at a loss. "In the pantry?"

"Bring a candle," Elie advised. Already he felt more alert, less heavy and hollow. Drat. He had to stop forgetting meals.

There were two unlit candles on the table, waiting to light

Brine and Elie to bed. Brine lit one at the kitchen fire and turned, arm crooked for Miss Turner to take. She had already stalked ahead of him into the narrow pantry; he followed her in and shut the door.

Leaving the room had clearly been an effort at tact or privacy or both, but the wall was thin and Brine's hearing imperfect. Elie could make out nearly the whole of the conversation. Going upstairs without saying goodnight seemed rude, and—

And he was desperately curious.

"…I pay Mr. Eleazar to look after my affairs in my absence," Brine was saying. "He's only trying to make sure you're looked after, if I—have to leave you. Couldn't you see you hurt his feelings? I *asked* him to explain why we shouldn't wait any longer, and he did."

"Yes, he explained I would get more money from you that way. One presumes that is the basis on which he conducts his own association with you. You had better let me look over your account with him."

"If he hoped to make a profit from me, he has been sorely disappointed," Brine snapped. "I owe him money."

"Which he will collect from your prize share," she said, exasperated. "Honestly, Augie, you're like a babe in the wood. Next you'll tell me you have a will in his favor."

Elie smiled slightly; here he would be speedily exonerated. He'd helped Brine update his will after the elder Mr. Brine's death. It would need updating again to provide for any children of his marriage, but if Brine died tomorrow—Heaven forbid—then Miss Turner would get everything.

"Yes," Brine said in what he probably thought was a furious undertone. "I have a will in his favor."

9

Apple cake stuck in Elie's throat. Hastily, he guzzled tea. He couldn't choke now, or he'd miss the rest of the conversation!

"I see," Miss Turner said triumphantly.

"Of course you shall have the bulk of it," Brine hurried to add. "There may not be much, after my debts are paid, but—"

"How do you even *know* what your debts are, except that Mr. Eleazar tells you?"

Elie's punishment fit his crime, at least.

"I am not quite hopeless at arithmetic," Brine said coldly.

"I never said you were. I mean, how can you know he quotes you honest prices?"

"Christ, Sarah—"

"Don't take the Lord's name in vain."

"I beg your pardon, but the idea of him cheating me is absurd. If that was what he wanted, I have certainly given him plenty of opportunity, and instead he convoys me to a frankly humbling extent. I was dead drunk on Sunday, and he fetched me out of…" He trailed off.

"Let me guess," said Miss Turner. "A gin-shop."

"Yes, if you must know. And then he made me a sandwich and read to me out of *The Seaman's Guide and Coaster's Companion.*"

"He…what?"

Elie flushed at Miss Turner's bemusement, palpable even through the wall.

Brine lost his patience. "You talk as if advancing me money were some trick of his. But what it really means, Sarah, is that I have the use of the money, and he does not! Do you know how many men desert with their agents' money in their pockets? And their outstanding pay and prize money goes straight to Greenwich Hospital, leaving the agent with a worthless receipt."

"All the more reason for agents to pad their bills," Miss Turner said. "Honestly, Augie, I *should*—" She was clearly about to say *I should marry you, and look after your affairs.* Elie waited dully.

"Why shouldn't he have my watch to remember me by?" Brine interrupted. "He bought me the damn thing."

Emotion surged in Elie's chest, rushing up his throat and pressing against his skull, like the sea trying to smash through a dike. His ears popped.

"You mean he *sold* you the watch, Augie," Miss Turner said with the same tolerant scorn, as though nothing at all had changed. "Kindly remember that I am not a sailor, to be overawed by coarse language. But if it's only the watch, I suppose there's no harm in it."

Some creaking and rustling. "I said he might take what he liked from my personal effects," Brine said—or Elie thought he did. He was speaking more softly, evidently embarrassed. "And—well—a few odds and ends for the children. I thought the eldest Miss Lazarus might like to have my hat. Do you remember when I bought it? I sent you a drawing, I think, of her wearing it."

There was a long pause. "Yes," Miss Turner said slowly, in a less superior voice. "You drew a face on the hat as if it were her head. Yes, I do remember that. So—you have left your agent your keepsakes, and me your money. That is rather backwards, don't you think?"

Dead silence. "To be perfectly honest, I didn't expect you to *want* my belongings," Brine said, in the tone of a man backed into a corner. "The watch is the only thing among them that would look out of place in an ash-heap."

Elie, having supplied most of the belongings in question, felt stung, and hoped Miss Turner wouldn't seize upon the point.

"And you've never exactly been sentimental," Brine continued. "If you write me four times a year, it's more than—"

"And how often does Mr. Eleazar write you?"

There was a clatter, and something rolled across the floor. An apple or an onion, probably. "He's my agent. A frequent correspondence is—"

"It sounds to *me* as if he were your friend."

Elie held his breath. Would Brine be allowed, finally, to finish a sentence?

"We've wandered rather far from the subject, haven't we?" Brine said at last. Elie's heart sank at his tone—low and intimate, with a warm dip in it. "*You* are my oldest and dearest friend in the world, Sarah."

"Don't crowd me," said Miss Turner, without conviction.

"Haven't I a right to provide for you? Of course I've left you my money. I care for you, and you need it."

"But I don't. I don't want your money, Augie. I just want you to live. I want you to live and come home. That's all."

The floorboards creaked again. "I know," Brine said tenderly. "I don't want to argue with you, Sarah. I don't understand why we're fighting about Eleazar Benezet, of all people, when we have so little time together."

Elie flushed hot. *Eleazar Benezet, of all people.* As though he and his letters—his love letters, not to put too fine a point on it—were one of those trivialities married people were always quarreling over when they were really angry about something else entirely.

Jael and her governess had had a passionate public argument about guitars, of all things. Jael's had been lost in the fire, so she'd decided to buy the plainest, cheapest one in Rye, just until she could go to London and have a better selection. Miss Oliver seemed to have taken it as a slight on herself, and suddenly they had been looking daggers at one another and jockeying to be the first to stalk proudly out of the shop.

Leaving Elie behind to actually buy the blasted guitar, of course. It was as ludicrous for him to send Brine love letters as it would have been for the guitar to ask Jael to woo it before taking it home.

There was a thud, as though one of them had knocked into a shelf. Brine gave a low laugh. "Sorry, let me pick up that onion."

Their voices sank to murmurs. As Brine's hearing had not suddenly improved, they must have moved closer together.

Elie lit his candle and went upstairs before he had to hear the murmurs die away too.

WEDNESDAY, 29 SEPTEMBER / 5 TISHREI
MICHAELMAS

Traditional wardroom toast:
"Ourselves—as no one else is likely to concern
themselves with our welfare."

Elie listened for Brine's footsteps to go down the stairs, planning to wait a few minutes before following. If Brine got Elie alone on the landing, he'd want to talk about last night's conversation with Miss Turner.

There was a tentative rap on his door. He ignored it.

"Mr. Eleazar?" Brine said softly. Elie kept his eyes on the clock. Just a little more patience.

Brine waited exactly half a minute before continuing down to breakfast. That seemed too round a number to be pure chance. Had he, too, been counting the seconds?

Why shouldn't he have my watch to remember me by?

It made Elie's whole chest hurt, to think about Brine writing his will. Before a battle, maybe, or after one, or shaken by the news of a friend's death. Going through his own things one by one, deciding who might like to have each. (Even if he'd decided none of them were fine enough for Miss Turner!)

Elie firmly believed that everyone ought to have a will. *It's not bad luck,* he'd urged clients a thousand times. *It's the opposite. It protects the people you love.* But it struck him now how paltry an amulet it really was, how flimsy and superstitious: ritually dividing your possessions as if that could shield your loved ones from loss.

I just want you to live, Augie, Miss Turner had said, as though Brine could do it if he would only make an effort.

Please, Elie prayed, lips numb, *inscribe Brine in the Book of*

Life, and mãe, and Aunt Hava, and… He ran through the names of his family, one by one, and felt an absurd panic when he could only remember three of his cousin Batseba's five children.

He'd tarried upstairs too long, trying to avoid Brine. When he got to the kitchen, the only empty chair was next to Brine's. Elie took it with a cheerful good morning, helping himself from the toast rack.

"I'm sorry about what Miss Turner said last night," Brine whispered, loudly enough for the whole table to hear.

Elie frowned vaguely. "Which thing? I'm afraid I can't remember…" He took a large bite of toast.

Brine glanced round at the listening Lazaruses and subsided, looking defeated.

The dry mouthful scraped Elie's throat going down. "I'm sure it was nothing to worry about. Just part of the job."

"It shouldn't be."

Elie shrugged. "We were all tired last night—probably Miss Turner most of all. Thanks for making me that cup of tea."

Brine gave him a small smile. "Where are you off to this morning?"

"The dockyard, to collect my clients' Michaelmas pay and allotments. I need to stop by the rope yard while I'm there, too, on behalf of the *Unicorn*'s purser."

Brine's brows drew together. "You take an escort, don't you?" Elie stared at him. "You can't go to the Pay Office on your own, and come away with God knows how much cash."

Everyone had already been listening, but now they gaped openly. "I go with him," Samuel said.

"That makes twice as much cash, then."

"Not really. My business is much smaller."

"The cashiers mostly give banknotes these days," Elie said. "It's not as though my pockets will be bulging with sovereigns. I carry a boatswain's whistle, just in case."

"Then you're worried."

"It's to please my mother. I've never had to use it."

I'm safer walking through Portsmouth than I am coming alongside your beloved Steadfast, he didn't say. And he would never in a million years say *When a navy agent and his wife were assaulted on their own doorstep a few years back, it was Royal Navy officers who did it.*

Brine crossed his arms. "I should go with you."

"Afraid I'm hiding sharp practice from you?" Elie asked mildly. "I'd be happy to open my books for Miss Turner if it would ease your mind."

The room fell absolutely silent. Shame and regret washed over Elie at the look on Brine's face.

Gracia popped out from under the table between her parents' chairs. "What's sharp practice?" When no one answered, she repeated it louder.

Lottie set her fork down with a click. "It means 'cheating,' Gracie."

Aunt Hava tried to smooth things over. "Ai, meu Eleazar, if the boy wants to be an unpaid bodyguard, what's the harm?"

"Yes, I shouldn't have—" Elie began.

"Uncle Elie, did Miss Turner accuse you of cheating?" Lottie looked genuinely upset.

"No, no. Of course not."

"She did, didn't she? Why are people so spiteful? Just when that horrible January woman finally stopped petitioning to have your license withdrawn." She glared at

Brine, who looked a bit sick. "Her horrible son was too embarrassed to tell his mother he'd spent all his money on women, so he blamed the shortfall on Uncle Elie. The most honest person I know!"

Her father laughed. "Thanks, minha filha."

Elie felt extremely undeserving of this praise. "Miss Turner didn't accuse me of anything, Lottie. Don't fret about me. I don't know why I said what I did. I must still be half-asleep. Brine, please forgive me—"

"No, *I* apologize," Brine said. "Most humbly. I never meant to impugn your honor, but of course my suggestion was impertinent. A habit of command is no excuse—"

"For the love of—" Elie threw up his hands. "Brine. You were kind, and I was petty. You know that. I'm not an officer, to challenge you to a duel for worrying about me." Then he wished he hadn't said *officer* in quite that tone. But Brine's shoulders relaxed.

"Or for anything else, really," Elie continued in relief. "In extreme cases, a lawsuit is much less messy. Quieter, too. Well, quieter in the short term. Possibly in the aggregate—"

Brine started to smile. "But what if I say something really unforgivable?"

Did he know how intimate his voice sounded? That warm dip in it? Elie smiled helplessly back. "Jews have a procedure for that."

"Yes, a lawsuit," Morris said dryly. Everybody laughed, even Lottie and poor obliging Brine.

"Well, what's the procedure?"

"First you beg for forgiveness." Elie strove to inject no intimacy whatsoever into that statement.

Brine's eyes glinted. "In any particular manner?"

Elie was glad his family was present, or he might have been tempted to answer (entirely inaccurately) *On your knees.* "Sincerely. Offering restitution if appropriate." Drat, had that sounded lewd to anyone else?

Brine leaned in. "And if you proved obdurate?"

"You apologize again," Lottie said, still a bit sharp. "In front of three friends."

"Whom you bring with you to attest to your repentance," Samuel explained.

"And to show you're willing to humble yourself," Leah added.

"If that doesn't work, you're supposed to go again with a minyan and grovel," Morris said. "Yes, Gracele, I'm cutting up another piece of toast for you right now. But then you have to go back to the children's table and finish your egg."

"I like them *thin,* tateh," Gracia reminded him.

"A minyan is—" Samuel began.

"Ten Jewish men, isn't it?" said Brine. "You need it to say certain prayers." Samuel looked surprised. "Once when I was here, you were all worried there might not be one for something or other. I offered to go, but Mr. Eleazar explained I wouldn't be of any use." Elie hoped he hadn't put it quite like that.

"Well, the idea is that God—HaShem hears your third apology," Samuel went on, "and if your repentance is sincere, hopefully He'll forgive you even if Elie doesn't."

"It doesn't really happen much these days," Elie said. "If it ever did."

"No, people are too stiff-necked," put in Rebecca. "With a lawsuit, you lose your money but keep your pride."

Elie kept his eyes on his toast. "Maybe they're too gracious. Maybe they accept the apology the first time, and everyone can forget about it."

Lottie snorted.

"So what *did* Miss Turner say to you?" Samuel asked as they took their place in the Pay Office queue curving up Queen Street along the dockyard's south wall. Sometimes the sunny bricks could be pleasant to lean on, but this morning they were cold to the touch. Everyone who could afford it was bundled up against the chill, and more than one half-pay lieutenant shivered in his threadbare uniform.

"Nothing too terrible," Elie said. "Not to my face, anyway. Brine asked me to explain the advantages of matrimony to her, and she was outraged when I said that widows get pensions and sweethearts don't. I couldn't really blame her."

"Ah. And behind your back?"

"Mostly that Brine was taking my integrity on faith, and that he'd never know it if I was price-gouging him, which…"

"Which he might not," Samuel finished. "Well, it'll serve her right if she makes him find a new agent and they're suddenly much poorer."

Elie felt hot despite the nip in the air. He tugged hopelessly at his muffler. "I make a hash of everything."

"It's one client," Samuel said gently. "Making a hash of it with one or two when you have hundreds isn't so bad."

He unwound the muffler and stuffed it in his pocket. "It feels like everything."

"I know, meu primo. I'm sorry." Samuel squeezed his shoulder. "Do you want me to take him on? I could still let him have things cheap, and you could pay me back."

"Thanks, but it's my problem. I'd better fix it myself."

Samuel gave him a shrewd glance. "If you say so."

"Sorry." He pulled his gloves off to press cold fingers to his cheeks. "I know how tiresome this must be."

"Being fond of people is always tiresome. Just wait till you have—sorry, I'm as bad as my mother. Take it from a man who has children."

Elie's throat hurt. Did Samuel know? Was he waiting for Elie to confide in him? That had been ambiguous, of course, and yet… But what could Elie say to him? Samuel looked so solid, so whole.

Elie would have liked to have children, honestly. But he wouldn't, not unless he inherited someone else's, as Uncle Simeon had inherited Elie. No one *hoped* for that.

Elie wasn't even at the head of the queue for testamentary guardian to his cousins' children. It didn't matter that he loved them, that he was steady, that he'd have more to leave his heirs than any of the Lazaruses or that he'd already promised years ago to give Lottie a dowry. It only mattered that he didn't have a wife.

He heard again Miss Turner's revulsion: *vulture.*

Elie knew he wasn't a vulture. So why was he choking on the taste of carrion—of other people's scraps?

He wanted to feel like a clerk again, like a pocket calendar, blank and unruffled and suited to his purpose. "Thanks," he said. "Have you heard of any new lieutenants' berths coming vacant?"

1 0

Elie filed away the last of his quarter-day business, and was on the point of pulling out the *Vliegende Draeck* papers when he realized he had forgotten to inquire about HMS *Unicorn*'s new rope. Had he better return to the dockyard? No, a messenger was good enough. He dispatched one.

But just as he was dropping the *Draeck* file onto his desk with a thump, Brine climbed the stairs with a carefree smile and a paper sack redolent of fried fish, as if this morning had never happened.

Which was exactly what Elie would like to pretend, too, so it was perverse of him to say, "Come to see if I made it home from the Pay Office in one piece?"

"I'm sure I don't know what you mean," Brine said, sitting on the edge of his desk and inspecting his teacup. Finding it cold, he dumped it out and refilled it. "I happened to be on the Point and thought you might have been too busy to order dinner." He produced an orange from his sack and set it on the desk, where it glowed like a jewel in the shadow of the *Vliegende Draeck* file. "How do you like them cut? Have you got a plate or a bit of waste-paper or something?"

Elie felt worn out and defenseless. Didn't Brine understand that Elie looked after himself fifty weeks a year, and that it was insulting to show up for the odd fortnight and imply Elie wasn't very good at it?

Except Brine looked after himself fifty weeks a year too, and Elie still wanted to… The list of things Elie wanted to do for Brine could paper Aunt Hava's house from cellar to attic, honestly.

He handed over an old newspaper. "In quarters, thanks. Listen, have I ever explained Yom Kippur to you?"

"It's a day of atonement," Brine said promptly. "And a fast."

"Yes," Elie said, charmed as always that Brine paid attention. "And that's because…you see, on Rosh Hashanah, the Holy One inscribes in the Book of Life everyone who'll survive the coming year. But He only affixes His seal to the list on Yom Kippur. Until then, there's a chance of Him changing His mind."

"So it's the last day to file an appeal, you mean?"

"Precisely. We spend this week in going over the last year: trying to set things right, to finish what we've left undone and to make amends to people we've wronged. If there is a judgment against us in Heaven, it can be reversed through repentance, righteousness, and prayer."

"Do you believe God answers prayers?" Brine's voice was subdued. Two swift, crisscross strokes of his pocketknife, and the fruit yielded to him with a sigh.

"I don't know." Orange flooded Elie's nostrils, sweet and fresh. He recalled Brine's salve, his own hands on Brine's back. His fingertips tingled. "But what can we do, except hope?"

Brine wiped his knife carefully on the newspaper, and pocketed it. "I'm not sure I do hope."

"Neither do I," Elie confessed. They stared at each other. "I miss it." His voice cracked.

Brine nodded. Elie couldn't stand it—this connection, this illusion of possibility crackling between them, when there was nothing to even hope *for*. He slid two slices of orange towards Brine, and two towards himself. *May they never meet.*

"I was explaining that, because…" Everything in Elie recoiled from even this small avowal—everything but a hard, hot, irreducible point in the center of his chest. "I hope you don't mind, but I've been praying for you. To be inscribed in the Book of Life, I mean. I don't think of you as an investment."

There was a long silence. Elie counted visible seeds in the orange slices neither of them had even reached for.

"I know you don't," Brine said. "I'm sorry for what Sarah said. I never should have dragged you into our argument. I wouldn't have exposed you to insult for the world."

"I accept your apology, and I'm sorry about this morning. I shouldn't have dragged my family into it, either, and I really didn't mean to."

Brine waved this away.

"Miss Turner cares about you. That's as it should be. And she doesn't know *me* from Adam."

Brine's fingertips twitched. Then he pushed away from Elie's desk and strode restlessly to the window. "I asked her to marry me when I was seventeen."

"I know."

"But you don't really." Even when he turned away from the harbor to face Elie, he stood with one hip propped on the sill, leaning towards the sea. "She and I were friends when I left Birmingham. I didn't go home again until four years later—didn't even want to go then. I was always an undutiful son."

"It's hard to spend your leave on duty, when you get so little."

Brine shook his head. "My mother encouraged my visits to Sarah. She told me not to hurry home, and smiled. For four years, every letter was *How soon will you be home?* and then when I got there… But it wasn't as though I wished to hurry." He combed his hair back with his fingers, impatiently. "I'm not saying it well. Of course I didn't only call on Sarah to avoid my parents. I'd never talked to a young woman—a young lady—for more than five minutes at a time, and she'd grown breasts— And that's worse, isn't it?" He pressed his forehead to the glass. "She was the loveliest, purest thing I'd ever seen, and when she let me kiss her—" He cut himself off again, flustered. "Only a kiss. Nothing truly improper."

Tact would stretch this very predictable story to an hour. "If you have a secret child, we should change your will. Otherwise it's none of my business." Elie tried not to glance at the clock.

"It was all very innocent," Brine insisted. "But do you know how a boat will shake and jump in the water, and then you trim the sail just by an inch and she shoots forward straight and smooth? That's how I felt, when she let me kiss her."

Which could have meant almost anything, from *I wanted to believe I liked girls* to *I adored her passionately*. Did it even matter now? A new translation of one moment wouldn't alter the thirteen years that had come after.

Maybe that was what Brine was trying to explain.

"I should have married her then, when she was a sapling," he said savagely. His knuckles were white on the windowsill. "She'd have done it without arguing then, but I wasn't in the mood to hurry home. She's been waiting for me nearly half our lives. She gave up years, nursing my parents. You remember how long my father was ailing."

"I do. Miss Turner took very good care of him."

Brine's face softened. "She's an oak," he said fondly. "Of course she did. And now I've got to take care of her. What kind of man am I, if I don't?"

"If you think she's changed her mind," Elie said, trying to sound as dispassionate as a preprinted legal form, "you could offer her a settlement for breach of promise."

His mouth spasmed. "I asked her if she wanted me to release her," he said in a low voice. "I asked her if there was somebody else. She said no."

That was that, then. "All right. She must really be worried the prize money won't come through. It's understandable, after four years." Actually, it struck Elie as unaccountable. She claimed the money didn't matter, and then she refused to marry Brine without it, when she could have been his wife and sharing his bed tomorrow. Why? How could she resist?

But then, people *were* often unaccountable, and they did often think it would be more virtuous not to care about money, when in fact nearly everyone *had* to. Of course Miss Turner could not live on love and roses, even if she was too stiff-necked to admit it. Elie prefaced his next suggestion with, "I can't speak to your very understandable personal objections to delay." Was that adequate? It would have to be; it was already too close to Leah's arch remark about Miss Turner's impatience. "But as far as providing for Miss Turner out of your prize share is concerned, you can do that as soon as it's distributed, married or not. All you have to do is instruct me to make the money over to her; I can draw something up for your signature now."

"Thank you," Brine said. "I thought of that too, but then I thought I must be being stupid about shore matters again, because Sarah refused point-blank and told me it would be a scandal, and her dear departed father the vicar would spin in his grave, and everyone else would say she must be my mistress."

"But that's absurd!" Elie faltered. "Isn't it?"

Brine gave him a rather piercing look. "Entirely absurd, as to the truth. As to what the gossips in Birmingham might say, how the devil should I know?"

"I don't know what they might say either. That's all I meant, truly." Elie tried to formulate an appropriate apology for having indirectly and inadvertently implied that Brine and Miss Turner might possibly have done something perfectly harmless, natural, and commonplace (but which, of course, he himself would be miserable if they *had* done), and gave it up as a bad job. "We could make it out to be a bequest from a distant relation."

Brine's mouth curved tiredly. "You really are a dab hand with a loophole. But she'd never agree to anything like that."

Then don't tell her. Elie couldn't suggest that. *Dishonest,* Brine would call it, with perfect justice. *Dishonorable. Ungentlemanly. Beneath me.*

Brine buried his hands in his hair. "I don't know what to do."

But Elie knew exactly what to do. He had known all along; he only didn't want to do it. "It's actually quite simple. If you want to marry her, and she wants to marry you, and the only obstacle to your union is the *Draeck* distribution, then all you have to do is go away and let me work on the prize accounting."

Sliding the orange on its newspaper aside, Elie spread his pocket calendar flat with both hands, to hide their shaking.

"Your leave concludes on Friday, the eighth of October. Today is Wednesday, the twenty-ninth of September. I can't go up to London before Yom Kippur ends on Monday, but I'll finish the accounting by late Monday night and go straight to the mail coach. I'll write today to Captain Willing's prize agent, to ask him to be ready to submit the accounts first thing Tuesday morning. If the proctor certifies them promptly, I can be back here on the morning of the seventh or eighth with your money in hand." That might be long odds, but Elie could borrow the money from his uncle if he had to. "All you have to do is sort out the license while I'm gone. The dockyard chaplain gave me instructions; I'll write them up for you."

He took three guineas from his purse and set them on the corner of his desk. "This should cover the costs. I'll add it to your account." He kept his head bent over the calendar as Brine's feet crossed the room to stand beside his chair.

"I'm sorry," Brine said unhappily. The gold winked out like a candle as his hand closed over it. "I've really tried, all these years, not to make difficulties for you."

Elie quashed the mean urge to say *So you can handle the license on your own, then?* He stole a glimpse past the brim of his hat at Brine's beautiful, weather-beaten face. "You're not an investment. You don't have to pay dividends to be worthwhile. Miss Turner told you that too."

Brine flicked a glance over Elie's ledgers, his bundles of other people's papers, the stacks of receipts on their spikes. Then he opened his hand and let Elie's coins fan across his palm with a clink. "And you believe that, do you?" he said with startling cynicism.

Brine might as well have picked him up like a stray receipt and shoved him down on a spike. Elie hadn't expected to figure in this conversation at all. Now here he was, scanned from start to finish, neatly categorized, and transfixed.

He raised his head and met Brine's piercing eyes. His own crinkled fondly. "I believe it about you," he said lightly.

Brine's mouth tightened with something like anger. "All right. I'll do as you ask, and leave you to your work." He dropped the coins in his pocket. "Thank you."

When he was gone, Elie gave the orange to the porter's children.

Brine still seemed out of sorts that night at dinner. He passed over an open chair by Elie to sit across the table, and his impatience was palpable as Aunt Hava went through what felt like an entire Prize List of girls she planned to introduce Elie to on Sunday, when everyone went to the cemetery to pay their respects to the dead and remind them it was nearly Yom Kippur, and could they put in a good word for their surviving friends and relations?

Elie had been handling his family's matchmaking for years, but with Brine's tense face squarely in view, his usual aplomb deserted him. If he went along, Brine would think him spineless and over-dutiful. If he objected, things might be said that he would rather Brine not hear. There had already been one minor scene at breakfast. "I've already met Miss Franchetti," he said mildly. "Any number of times."

"Not recently," countered Aunt Hava. "She's grown into a real beauty. Morris, tell him."

"With my wife listening?" Morris joked. "Not likely."

Rebecca rolled her eyes. "Breasts to here." She gestured.

Lottie crossed her arms over her own bosom, which she seemed to believe kept growing purely to spite her. "You're all disgusting. Violet is nice, and clever, and really funny."

"Maybe Mr. Eleazar will like her," Brine said. From his startled flinch at Lottie's glare, he might have meant to say it under his breath. "Your pardon, Miss Lazarus, I only thought—"

"You thought everybody is desperate to get married just because *you* are."

Brine flushed a dull red.

"Lottie!" Elie said. Was she only out of charity with Brine and sensitive on the subject of marriage, or was she sweet on Violet Franchetti? "I know you're trying to defend me, but Mr. Brine is our guest and his remark was perfectly unobjectionable. I'm sure I *will* like Violet."

"Apologize to our guest, Lottie," Aunt Hava said.

"Oh, no," Brine protested. "Please don't—"

"I'm sorry," Lottie said in a stifled voice. "Making personal remarks about other people's private lives is extremely rude, and I should not have done it merely because everybody else was."

Elie could not quite swallow his bark of startled laughter. He hid behind his wineglass and then his napkin, but it was a minute or two before he regained his composure and emerged, ready to offer a round of apologies to the table.

But the storm seemed to have blown over. Everyone was smiling ruefully, and Aunt Hava changed the subject with, "You didn't make your toast tonight, Mr. Brine."

Standing, Brine raised his glass. "Ourselves, as no-one else is likely to concern themselves with our welfare."

To sailors and Jews as a class, the toast felt all too true. But as an individual, Elie had no excuse for that kind of self-pity. He was surrounded, in fact, by people who'd concern themselves with his welfare at the drop of a hat, whether he wanted them to or not.

So why did the wine taste so bitter on his tongue?

THURSDAY
Traditional wardroom toast:
"A bloody war or a sickly season."

In the morning, Elie managed to collate the *Vliegende Draeck* papers and draw up a preliminary expense account: court and copying fees, insurance, warehousing, agents' travel, auctioneers' wages, and so on. But after that, he had to put the file away again. Clients and their families would be in and out all afternoon collecting their Michaelmas pay, and the last thing he needed was to misplace any of the carefully sorted papers.

"…I'll certainly apply for that berth on the *Virgin Queen*," Lt. Cornish said as Elie showed him out after a lengthy discussion of his prospects. "Please do inform me if you should hear of any others. Thanks. By the way—" He turned his hat in his hands. "Do you know there's a woman outside asking questions about you?"

"What?" Had Alex January's mother come to make trouble again?

The lieutenant coughed. "I told her you were all aboveboard."

Elie groaned. He'd thought this was finally resolved! "What did she ask you?"

"Er…" Mr. Cornish cringed at the very mild edge in Elie's voice. Despite many sterling qualities, his was not a commanding personality. Privately, Elie feared he'd never see active duty again.

"Sorry. It's not you I'm annoyed with. But if you could just repeat—" Then he heard familiar voices in the stairwell. "Ah. Never mind."

Miss Turner appeared over the horizon. Brine followed in her wake, a chivalrous hand at the small of her back. That did *not* make Elie green with envy. He rose politely. "Is this the lady you spoke of?"

"Quite," Mr. Cornish said hastily. "Good day, sir, sir, madam." He squeezed past Brine with a respectful nod and clattered down the stairs.

Elie took a deep breath. "Good afternoon, Mr. Brine, Miss Turner. How may I be of assistance?"

Brine's jaw tightened. "I was just stopping by with dinner, and found Sarah making a pestilence of herself."

"I brought my dinner with me."

Miss Turner, unruffled, took a turn about the office, peering and poking at things.

Brine raised his eyebrows. "So you've already eaten, then."

"No," Miss Turner said behind him. "I should think not." Elie spun around to see her with his open pack, lifting a corner of the napkin he'd wrapped his dinner in.

He rushed over and shut the flap. "I was on the point of eating when— Miss Turner!" He plucked Lt. Cornish's signed pay-receipt out of her hand and stuck it on a spike, facedown. "If you cannot respect my and my clients' privacy, I shall have to ask you to leave."

"Sarah, for Christ's sake!"

"The Lord's name, Augie." But she took a chair and folded her hands in her lap. "May I see Mr. Brine's account, sir?"

Elie didn't want to show her, but what difference did it make, after all? She couldn't know the wholesale prices he entered in Brine's account were too low, not without a complete audit of his books neither she nor Brine were competent to perform. He took a step towards his secretary.

"No, she may not," Brine said in a voice of steel. "You've no right to see them, Sarah, and not only no right to inquire into Mr. Eleazar's conduct, but no possible cause. I will stake my honor on his probity."

This tack would probably be less effective here than it would have been in the wardroom (where to disagree any further would as good as provoke a duel), but emotion stopped Elie's throat. Oh, he had no right to be so moved—far less right, in fact, than Miss Turner had to suspect him. Brine's honor was everything to him, and Elie had just made him an unwitting liar.

Miss Turner smiled at her intended. "I can see that you would, Augie. But you must let me make up my own mind. Really! You would marry me, but not show me your bank-book?"

Brine's mouth softened. "I will make you a bargain: when we are married, you may see the bank-book."

"Bribery?" Miss Turner gave Brine a sly, sidelong glance. "*Tsk tsk.*"

This had gone on long enough. Elie sat in his own chair, drawing strength from the familiar tableau of desk and clients. "So, Miss Turner." Steepling his fingers, he regarded her serenely. "You have been making inquiries among my other clients. Collecting material for your complaint to George Rose?"

Her face was all innocence and confusion. "Who?"

"The Treasurer of the Navy," said Brine shortly.

"He has the power to revoke a navy agent's license for fraud or misconduct," Elie said. "I'll give you his address and a copy of the statute, if you like."

Miss Turner looked abashed. Brine crossed his arms and leaned against the mantel at the back of the room. "She doesn't like. Do you, Sarah?"

Miss Turner recovered. "I'm hardly some sort of Lady Macbeth. I simply…" She glanced at Brine, and Elie couldn't hold on to his anger. She simply felt responsible for Brine's welfare because she loved him. Who could understand that better than Elie? He should have learned his lesson about self-righteousness at breakfast yesterday, instead of giving an encore nobody had asked for and putting poor, steadfast Brine between the devil and the deep sea.

"Brine," he said, "I know it's asking a lot, but the dockyard has been dragging its feet giving the *Unicorn* her new rope, and I promised her purser I'd look into it. They've already fobbed off two messengers, and I don't know when I'll have time to go myself before I leave for London. You'd do me a great favor if you could stop by the rope yard and rattle your saber."

Brine's eyes narrowed.

Elie gazed limpidly back. He didn't think about Brine's hips, even if that pose drew attention to them. Why did he persist in *leaning* on things? Did he do it on purpose?

Brine shouldered himself upright with a roll of his spine, and the room shrank to half its usual size. "Fine," he said, voice thrumming with suppressed aggression. Was *that* on purpose? Elie could have sworn that sometimes anger made him brisker, less exuberantly sensual. But other times—now, for instance, as he crossed the room in three paces and set his hand on Miss Turner's chair—electricity crackled in the air around his shifting muscles. "I'll escort you out, Sarah."

Pink stained her cheeks. "Oh—er—no thank you, Augie," she said faintly. "I believe you said something about a cup of tea, Mr. Eleazar?"

"No," said Brine, still crackling. "He didn't."

Elie was impressed by her firmness of purpose. He himself had decided not to risk trying to stand and walk Brine to the door. "I don't mind," he said. "Honestly, Brine. She'll be your wife. Better to have it out now. And you really would be doing me an enormous service by seeing about the rope."

Brine's perfect mouth tightened. A wave of heat rolled up Elie's chest, his neck—

Brine gave a taut bow, tucked his hat under his arm, and went out.

II

Elie tried to catch his breath and smile unselfconsciously at Miss Turner.

She brushed her hair out of her flushed face. "I detest an overbearing man."

He burst out laughing. "Do you?"

She smiled grudgingly. "Well, perhaps I don't detest that one. Even so, he needn't think I'll be overborne."

"Always wise to begin as you mean to go on." Elie took out his watch and his dinner, and set them on the table. "Now, I can give you twenty minutes while I eat. If you'd like tea, there's an urn in the corner, or I can make a fresh pot—"

"No, no, I don't really want tea. I want to talk to you."

Elie took a tiny bite of his sandwich, trying to fix it in his mind that he couldn't talk with his mouth full or she'd be mortally offended.

"I must apologize again for my rudeness on Tuesday," she began. "I hope you did not overhear our conversation in your aunt's pantry."

Elie washed down his tiny bite with a tiny sip of soda-water. "Why, was it worse than what you said to my face?"

Her lips twitched. She leaned forward with a candid air. "I worry about Mr. Brine, that's all. He doesn't understand how things are on land, so he doesn't always notice when they aren't how they should be."

"That's one reason sailors employ navy agents to oversee their affairs." He set down the sandwich. "Why won't you marry him? Really?"

She looked incredulous. "Mr. Brine doesn't want to marry me. *You* must know that."

He remembered what she had said in the pantry: that he was Brine's friend. She thought Brine had confided in him. Well, Brine had. "I can assure you that he does," Elie said around the lump in his throat. "He cares for you deeply."

"I care for him too." She plaited and unplaited her fingers, frowning at him. "Deeply."

Then put me out of my misery, Elie thought.

"And that is really *your* honest opinion." She sounded perplexed. "That he wants to marry me."

It dawned on Elie that he could say no. He could give it as his opinion that Brine didn't want to marry her, but felt honor-bound to do so. Miss Turner was already wavering, already thinking of breaking it off. For a moment, temptation struck him speechless. It might be for the best—

I will stake my honor on his probity.

Brine was a client. He trusted Elie. He had unequivocally communicated his wishes. It was Elie's job to carry them out to the very best of his ability. "Why should you doubt it? He has told you so himself, a hundred times."

"I think I'll have that cup of tea after all." Abruptly, she stripped off her gloves and crossed to the urn.

Elie ate his sandwich and didn't think about any of it. *I am a pocket calendar. A cheerful, conscientious pocket almanac calmly eating its sandwich. I am not thinking about Augustus Brine spreading me open on my desk with casual authority, his hands smoothing my pages before he jams his pen right into me.*

He suddenly remembered that it was a sign of disrespect to sit while a lady was standing. With a silent curse, he got to his feet. Then, on impulse, he went to his secretary and retrieved a document from the *Draeck* file. He set it on his desk, facing Miss Turner's chair.

She came back with her tea. Elie waited for her to take her seat again before he did the same. "I know sometimes he seems like a clumsy puppy on land. But he isn't." He nudged the paper towards her. "Have you read Captain Willing's account of the *Vliegende Draeck*'s capture?"

"No."

He set his finger on Brine's name. "Start here, at 'great coolness and decision.'"

She regarded him quizzically. "You know it by heart?"

"I've had occasion to read it several times. As you are so fond of pointing out, this case has dragged on for years." He took another bite.

She inched her chair closer and leaned in, eyes meeting his squarely. "So why not drag it out a little longer, eh?"

Elie choked.

He groped for his soda-water, so lightheaded he heard the flask clacking against his teeth before he felt it. Had she guessed? Was she about to accuse him?

"I don't understand why Augie is in such a hurry all of a sudden," she finished absently, head bent over the log extracts. "Are you well, sir? I do hope you're not coming down with something."

"Quite well, thank you," Elie wheezed. "Time passes differently at sea, I believe. I doubt he realized how much time *had* passed, and then he turned thirty, and a friend of his died and left a sweetheart in difficult circumstances…" Drat, that wasn't complimentary enough. And should he pretend to believe that of course *she* was much younger than Brine?

But she said, "Oh, I see," as if perfectly satisfied. "That clears it up, doesn't it? Thank you." Turning her full attention to Captain Willing's statement, she read it through twice, slowly, turning one of Elie's paperweights in her fingers—his favorite, a sea-worn pottery shard with a ship on it.

Then she set it down, straightened it so the horizon was level, and fixed her keen eyes on Elie. "What do you think of the state of Mr. Brine's career, Mr. Eleazar? His chances for promotion?"

He swallowed a sly remark about her vaunted disinterest in money. "As far as rank, a ship's master is already at the top of his profession. A larger ship would mean a higher salary, but possibly be disadvantageous as to prize-taking. But as yet I am aware of no wish on Mr. Brine's part of leaving the *Steadfast*, beyond the odd joke about the North Sea climate. Has he spoken of it to you?"

"No. That is very like him, to care more for being of service to Captain Hope than for his own career."

"Ambition isn't everything."

"As Caesar learned to his cost." Miss Turner's fingertip traced the paperweight's edge. She had hard-working hands, despite her wealth of allusions that went straight over Elie's hat.

"If you're concerned that his income won't stretch to a family—children—"

"Children!" She snorted. "Just what Mr. Brine needs, a pack of dependents without any useful naval connections." She regarded him with something like disappointment. "I do *wish* you would talk sense."

If she was sincere—or fishing for a compliment—then he should contradict her. On the other hand, if she was maneuvering to jilt Brine without appearing selfish, then he shouldn't. But how was he supposed to know which it was? Was there some signal he'd know how to read if he were a Gentile? He wished she would stop watching him so closely.

"All right, let's set all that aside for the moment," she said. "Masters can be promoted to shore appointments, can't they? They manage dockyards, and so on?"

Oh. Oh, that would hurt soon. But for the moment, it was too sweet to resist. Brine managing a dockyard someday was Elie's most secret wish, on the rare occasions when he indulged rosy daydreams of an impossible future. Brine would be stout and bustling and breathtakingly competent. Everyone would revere him, and make up to Elie in hopes of patronage, because it would be common knowledge that he was Brine's right hand. "Which dockyard would you want, if you could have any of them?"

She tapped a finger pensively on the desk, smiling. "I'm tempted to say Gibraltar, but I suppose one would tire of the heat eventually. One of the shipbuilding ones, I think. Chatham, perhaps, where they built the *Victory*."

"A fine choice," Elie admitted. "Sheerness has a better harbor and finer views, and once they finish rebuilding, it will be more rationally laid out. But it's bound to be a headache for the next ten years at least." It would be shiny and new just when Brine might begin to think of a shore appointment, in other words; he hoped she would take the point. "You need a patron to help you to a post like that, though."

"Yes, of course." *Tap tap* went her finger. "How does one acquire a patron?"

"Luck, mostly. Someone important happening to notice your talent and take a liking to you." He refolded Captain Willing's statement. "Being mentioned in dispatches never hurts."

"Mr. Brine is extravagantly capable of making people like and admire him. He needs managing in other ways, however. Yes, yes, I know, you're too cagey to agree. But you managed him very neatly a moment ago, nevertheless." She straightened the stack of papers beneath the paperweight. "*You* have naval connections, don't you?"

Elie's head spun. "Not at that level. My uncle does, to a small extent."

"Would they assist Mr. Brine, do you think?"

Had she really progressed so swiftly and brazenly from accusing him of picking Brine's pocket to asking for his help with Brine's career? But of course Elie had always meant to introduce Brine to Uncle Simeon at the first opportunity.

Maybe it would all work out beautifully. Maybe in a few years he'd be over his infatuation, and be unreservedly glad to be called *Uncle Elie* by Brine and Miss Turner's adorable children.

"Maybe," he said.

She began to pull on one glove, then frowned and pulled it off again. Digging in her reticule, she produced a bar of salve with an all-too-familiar label.

"I thought you made your own salve."

Her head snapped up. "What did you say?"

Elie blinked. "I said, I thought you made your own salve. Mr. Brine swears by it." *I shall smell cardamom and orange peel on my deathbed,* he didn't say.

She relaxed. "Oh. So I do. I forgot mine at home. I bought this at, er— I ran into you coming out of a shop…?"

"The sign of the Bulldog," Elie said glumly. "You can't buy All Hands On Deck anywhere else, because the Bulldog absolutely refuses to wholesale it."

"Is that unusual?"

"It's annoying," Elie said. "I can't *blame* him for wanting to drive up the price and keep all the profits—at least, if he's dealing fairly with the manufacturer. But every time someone asks me to sell them a bar and I can't… Uch."

She inspected her hands, then smelled them, looking skeptical. "People really ask you about this salve?"

"It's very popular." *Men swear by it for buggery.* Elie didn't think about it, and didn't blush. "Is there something wrong with it?" he asked hopefully.

She shrugged and pushed the bar towards him. "Judge for yourself."

He rubbed a little on the back of his hand. It went on smoothly, but… "The stuff you make Brine smells better."

She gave him a hard look.

Suddenly, Elie was thinking about it. His face flamed. What was wrong with him? There was nothing incriminating in what he'd said.

"Thank you. Cardamom would raise the price of the bar, I expect." She tilted her head as she worked her fingers into her glove. "And you think you would deal more fairly with the manufacturer of All Hands On Deck than Mr.—the Bulldog?"

"I'd have to look at the contract to be sure," Elie hedged. "But I wouldn't be surprised if the Bulldog secured advantageous terms for himself before the salve was in demand, and has stuck to them." He sighed. "I daresay I could sell twice as much of the stuff in Portsmouth alone, merely by supplying it to more traders. Taking into account the other ports—"

"But you think the manufacturer would be justified in breaking the original agreement, simply because he has made money in the interim?"

Elie considered. "Well, he might owe the Bulldog compensation of some kind for doing so. But it's very difficult to enforce specific performance of a contract for anything but the sale of real property. Contracts are founded on consent, and most really good ones—good for *both* parties—include provisions for terminating them. Setting aside the legal aspect and looking at the question from a purely moral point of view, I'm sure we agree that it is a good general rule to keep one's promises. But every rule has its exceptions. A gentleman may believe the mere fact of having given his word to be sufficient justification for an otherwise unjustifiable course of action, but my own opinion is that one can no more be morally obligated to fulfill a fundamentally unjust contract than to obey an—"

He broke off with a jolt. Lulled by her avid attention, he'd drifted into answering her almost as if she'd been Lottie quizzing him on the *Lex Mercatoria*. Now he realized that his words had been not only indiscreet, but subject to quite another interpretation.

Her eyes gleamed. "Which unjust laws did you have in mind, Mr. Eleazar? There are, after all, so many."

"I beg your pardon, ma'am, for rambling on. Of course you are not really interested in my opinions on contracts." Did she know Elie had suggested a breach of promise settlement? If Brine hadn't told her *yet*, might he do so later? How much would she resent it? "We *are* only speaking of wholesaling contracts, aren't we? I was. That is, I meant absolutely no veiled allusions." Sweat beaded on his forehead. Should he have pretended it hadn't occurred to him? "And I hope you won't think I treat my own obligations lightly. On the contrary, I take them very seriously indeed."

She smiled—too brightly? "Just so. We were merely making conversation." Her chair screeched on the floor. "And there, that's my twenty minutes." She popped the salve back into her reticule and stood. "I am so glad that you appear to have Mr. Brine's best interests at heart. If you turn out not to, naturally I shall do everything in my power to ruin you. I hope that is quite understood."

Elie's jaw dropped.

Her smile's luminosity increased by several degrees. "But that is also a pure hypothetical. God grant it may be as inapplicable to our circumstances as your remarks on wholesaling contracts. I shall not require the Treasurer of the Navy's direction at this time. I beg your forgiveness again for my previous aspersions. I hope there is no ill feeling, and that henceforward you and I will get on like a house afire."

Elie brushed aside a memory of Jael's home, still smoldering. "That would be a great weight off my mind," he said, wishing it felt truer. He had wanted Miss Turner to like him. Why couldn't he be satisfied, now that she seemed to? Maybe it was only her metaphor that had unsettled him. "Thank you, I accept your apology. Your concern for Mr. Brine was very natural." He rose and walked her to the door.

"Thank you for your patience, Mr. Eleazar. It has been illuminating." She marched down the stairs without a backwards glance.

12

FRIDAY

SHABBAT SHUVAH BEGINS AT SUNSET

Traditional wardroom toast:
"A willing foe and sea-room."

Elie sat down at last to finish the *Vliegende Draeck* accounting once and for all, and simply could not concentrate.

He made basic arithmetic mistakes. He misplaced receipts, searched for ten minutes, and found them at his elbow. He squinted at his paper. Was the day really so dark, or did the window need washing? His chair was hard, his collar itchy. His ink refused to flow smoothly, even after opening a fresh bottle and trimming his pen seven or eight times. His hat kept slipping.

He had almost talked himself into washing the window when rain began to patter insistently on the roof. It ran down the eave and dripped onto the iron cellar door, an irregular, impatient *tap, tap,* like Miss Turner's finger on his desk.

Why not drag it out a little longer, eh?

Elie lit a lamp and hunched over his blotter—and twenty minutes later found himself staring at the water running down the windowpanes, and fretting over whether the roads would be muddy on Monday night. He had only managed to copy another half a column of figures.

There had been a few messages in this morning's post that really ought to be replied to at once—and he owed his mother those new year's wishes. Maybe that would dissipate his torpor.

Then it was noon, and Elie had to either take a luncheon and admit he had wasted his morning, or go on working without refreshment and grow sluggish. He choked down a ship's biscuit and a cup of tea and waited in vain to feel refreshed.

Why couldn't he wake up? His work was rarely fascinating, and yet he managed to do it, and do it well. With energy, even. Was he doing this on purpose somehow, to stop Brine's marriage? Brine *trusted* him…

Elie shook himself—managed to stand and stretch—then spent ten minutes at the window watching the clouds scud over the sea, his forehead pressed to the glass just where Brine's had been two days ago. *She was the most beautiful thing I'd ever seen.*

He wondered if brisk Miss Turner ever felt as though her limbs were too heavy to lift.

With a convulsive effort, Elie opened the window and stuck his head out to clear it. Brine was striding down the street with as much energy as ever, his posture making no concession to the rain.

Elie's heart jumped—but heavily, late, like a dozing theatergoer poked by his neighbor at some thrilling development. Maybe he would never feel cheerful or awake again. Maybe he had smothered the part of himself that lived and laughed and lusted, and now it was dead.

Yet he straightened and smiled reflexively at Brine's entrance, his dull panic actually receding; deception had become so habitual that it no longer required conscious effort.

Brine had found the *Unicorn*'s rope.

It had been hidden at the back of a shed, presumably for diversion to another ship out of turn. Brine, having met with no success the day before, had reappeared this morning with a wagon and a few men from the *Steadfast*, and insisted that the clerk of the rope yard poke about with him. When Brine's hearty, backslapping obstinacy had shown no sign of flagging two hours later, the clerk had grudgingly "discovered" the rope, which was being rowed to the *Unicorn* at this very moment.

"Thank you," Elie said inadequately, feeling ready to weep with exhaustion and gratitude. Brine had performed the latter part of these heroics in the rain, and his hair curled with a vengeance, standing out from his head like a silver-gilt halo in the gray light.

"It was no trouble," Brine said with a blatant disregard for fact. He nudged some papers aside and leaned against Elie's desk, one foot on the floor and the other propped on the edge of the same chair Miss Turner had sat in. His interlaced fingers twisted nervously in his lap, just where Elie least wished his own eyes to stray. "What did Sarah say to you yesterday? I did get her promise not to write to George Rose. I don't know what in the seven hells she could complain of to him without perjuring herself, but—she promised."

"Thank you," Elie said again. "But she apologized for her suspicions, as it happens, and…"

She hinted that I should delay the prize distribution, said you needed managing, and inquired after your chances for a shore appointment would set the cat among the pigeons very thoroughly. Elie was deeply ashamed of the impulse. "I think you had better ask her directly."

"I did ask her."

Elie met Brine's eyes, and then wished he hadn't. He was amazed at how firm his voice sounded, when he said, "I can tell you she was mostly civil, and that I did my best not to repeat anything you had told me in confidence. Beyond that— I'm sorry, but you must see that go-between would be an unnavigable position for me. In your private life you'll have to shift for yourself, I'm afraid."

Brine's gaze fell. He gave a jerky nod. "Of course. I know I've been very selfish."

"I never said—"

"No, you didn't. But I have been. I wish I knew how to be less so. Every course seems equally disastrous."

Elie could feel the current dragging him towards the whirlpool of doubt and speculation: *What does he mean? Maybe he feels as you do—*

"I've been turning over what you said to me a couple of days ago," he said. "When you implied that I myself didn't see my own value, beyond the dividends I yielded."

Brine went still. "And…?"

"I—don't say you're entirely wrong. But it's a little more complicated than that." He ran his tzitzit between his fingers. "My father died when I was a very small child."

"Yes," Brine said softly. "I remember. Rotten luck."

"Uncle Simeon sent us a check every quarter for my maintenance. A father is responsible for his children's maintenance, but an uncle owes his nephew precisely nil, legally speaking." He ignored Brine's sound of protest. "He also offered to adopt me, and give my mother an annuity. I don't honestly know the details, or maybe I just don't remember them anymore. But I know mãe said *No, thank you* when she could have said yes. I would have been happy enough with Uncle Simeon and Aunt Alice and my cousins. And mãe would have been a merry, independent widow, instead of raising a son alone on someone else's money."

Brine's frown was deepening with every sentence. Here he opened his mouth.

"I'm sure you're imagining me as a meek little boy doing sums for my keep," Elie said bluntly. "But I wasn't. Oh, every now and then I worried mãe would change her mind. When I was first an errand boy at Benezet & Sons, there were a few days when everything went wrong and I was afraid I was a disappointment and a nuisance and the checks would stop coming. But mostly, I was—am—grateful."

"You talk as if it were charity!" Brine burst out. "One imagines that your mother liked having you about."

Elie smiled. "Yes, I—think that's my point, actually. There's a difference between a business connection and a personal one."

Brine drew back, face going blank. "Ah."

Elie remembered him asking, in that curiously intent voice, *If you despised me, would I know it?* What did Brine want from him? Elie didn't really see how he could make his feelings any more plain without shoving Brine down on the desk and kissing him senseless. And even if Brine wanted that—which seemed doubtful at best—there could be *no* doubt he considered it a selfish temptation he was honor-bound to resist.

"What I mean is," Elie forged on, "my family chose to take pains with me, when it would have been simpler and easier not to. They did it out of—there's a Hebrew word, chesed. It's usually translated as 'loving kindness.' I'm proud of repaying their pains. I'm proud of having the means now to do deeds of loving kindness in my turn, for people I care for. There's a difference between a debt to a friend, and a debt to a business associate. There's a difference between doing a friend a service, and fulfilling a contractual obligation." Elie groped for words. There was something important here, he knew there was. "Or there should be. I—I don't mean…"

"What *do* you mean?" Brine demanded.

Elie sighed. "I wish I knew. Sorry. I think—I think I mean that your friends want you to be happy." Yes, that was it. He wanted Brine to be happy. A weary sort of peace descended. "Your friends don't want your money, or your joyless duty. They want you to do what will make you happy— fundamentally, anyway. If they don't, then they're selfish, not you."

Brine crossed his arms. "Fine words, but it seems to me *your* family would settle for you marrying Violet Franchetti."

Elie shrugged. "I didn't say your friends *know* what will make you happy. I just meant—it isn't selfish or a sin, to consult your own preferences in the arrangement of your own life." He stood. "You've told me in no uncertain terms, more than once, that you want to marry Miss Turner. You've told me that if you can't, you'll be miserable. If you've changed your mind, then give me new instructions. If you haven't, then stop taking up my time while I'm trying to do your prize accounting." He went to the door.

Brine bit his cheek. He looked angry—or was it anger? Whatever it was, it was barely leashed. "And you'll follow my instructions, whatever they may be," he said softly.

"That's what you pay me for."

"Arguably, I haven't paid you much of anything yet."

Elie's heart pounded. "But you will, when you get your prize money." He put his hand on the doorknob.

Brine's eyes flashed. His hand covered Elie's, suddenly, holding the knob still. "Which is this? A business connection or a personal one?"

"If we're friends," Elie said sharply, raising his voice over the drumming in his ears, "then surely that's a double reason why I should do as you have repeatedly asked me. Have you changed your mind?"

There was a charged pause, and Brine let go and jammed his hat on his head. The light that tedious hours at the dockyard had failed to dim seemed to have gone out of him, all at once. "I'm sorry. I don't know what came over me. I'll try to be less ungrateful." Was that a note of sarcasm in his voice, or only weariness? His retreating footsteps were slower and heavier than his arriving ones had been.

Elie collapsed into the nearest chair. A thin, damp line etched itself into his trousers where Brine had balanced the sole of his shoe.

Elie had acted honorably and wisely, hadn't he? So why did he feel so cold and alone?

But he had told Brine he meant to work on the prize accounting, and he couldn't stand to be any more of a hypocrite than he was already. He loosened his itchy collar and forced himself doggedly back to his own hard chair. He trimmed the lamp, and copied one figure, then another.

Little by little, the personal side of things receded from his consciousness. His eyes sharpened, and his brain cleared. He built up the account in his head as a watchmaker assembled the movement of a watch, each spring and wheel balanced delicately in its place until the plate could be screwed on to secure it.

And just as he began to feel that he knew precisely what to do and had only to keep on doing it until it was done, little Kaatje came to fetch him for synagogue.

Elie looked at the *Vliegende Draeck* papers spread over his desk, each a carefully balanced cog. Shabbat Shuvah was beginning, and then Sunday would be Kol Nidre, then Yom Kippur on Monday, and he'd promised Brine he'd catch the Monday night mail coach. He'd wasted another day, and now he'd have to go on drafting the account in snatches between services and try to finish it on the journey instead of sleeping, and then make a fair copy as soon as he was off the swaying coach Tuesday morning, and by the end of it he'd be sick from too much coffee.

For a moment, Elie actually considered staying in his office. He could pay the fine for working on a holiday, if he was called to account for it.

"Vó says to come *now*, Uncle Elie," Kaatje said, already agitated at the prospect of failing in her appointed task.

Drearily, he piled the papers into a crate, laying tissue paper between each set of documents as if that could keep the whole intricate mechanism from collapsing in on itself. Then he extinguished the lamp and followed Kaatje down the stairs.

SATURDAY

S H A B B A T   S H U V A H

"Wives and sweethearts—may they never meet!"

The rabbi was preaching his annual sermon on repentance. The text was Psalm 51:12: Lev tahor b'ra-li

Elohim; v'ruach nachon, chadesh b'kirbi. *Create in me a clean heart, God, and renew within me a steadfast spirit.*

The word *steadfast* felt like a sign, maybe even a warning. He remembered Lottie saying he was the most honest person she knew, and Brine saying he would stake his honor on Elie's probity. All Elie wanted, all he had ever wanted, was to deserve their trust.

Except he wanted a great many other things, didn't he—most of them to do with Augustus Brine. Everything seemed murky and shifting like the waves before a squall, and tomorrow night HaShem would affix His seal to the Book of Life and close the gates to petitioners. Elie was meant to put things right this week, and instead he'd compounded every error. He'd wasted the Days of Repentance just like all the days before them.

He saw Brine only briefly, at dinner. Miss Turner had been invited too, and offended Aunt Hava by trying to pay for the food as though it were a public house.

"What's today's toast?" Zach asked after the Kiddush.

There was a pause. Brine stood and raised his glass in Miss Turner's direction, too heartily. A drop of wine sloshed over the brim and ran down the side of the glass. "To wives and sweethearts!" He drank precipitously. Elie could see his ears turning red.

"And the rest of the wardroom responds, 'May they never meet,'" Leah explained to her son.

Miss Turner snorted.

"The idea being that married officers wish to keep their mistresses secret," Leah continued. "I hope when *my* sons are grown, they will show their wives more respect."

"Yes, mamã," Zach said impatiently.

Brine wiped the spilled wine from his fingers, looking ready to sink into the floor. "I meant no disrespect, ma'am. Sarah."

"Oh, make up my plate and don't tie yourself in knots, Augie," Miss Turner said, not unkindly. "Of course I didn't expect you would live like a monk for thirteen years."

Brine's jaw clenched. He glanced at Elie—who alone at the table knew that Brine *had.* For a horrifying moment, Elie half expected to be called upon to testify that Brine had never bought a French letter.

"Sarah, let's talk about this later," he muttered.

"We really needn't. Oh yes, thank you, Mrs. Morris, I will have some chicken. It smells delicious."

Elie felt an unexpected stab of sympathy for Brine, who had taken a book to his freezing bed while other men enjoyed human companionship. So many efforts of will, so many tiny sacrifices made day by day and year by year—made with love and hope, like stitches in a bridal quilt—and now to find the gift had never been expected, and was of no particular use!

Brine was silent for the rest of dinner.

Jews' Burial Ground, Southsea
SUNDAY
YOM KIPPUR BEGINS AT SUNSET
"Absent friends."

"Violet, you remember my nephew Eleazar Benezet," Aunt Hava said with affectionate pride. "He works for his uncle Mr. Simeon Benezet, of Benezet & Sons."

Violet Franchetti had indeed grown up to be beautiful and buxom and very funny, and Elie didn't want to waste her time. To avoid any appearance of a snub, however, he settled in for five or ten minutes of friendly conversation before he could offer to fetch her a drink, giving some other young man an opportunity to swoop in.

This whole matchmaking business would always be a bit awkward, but Elie was used to it. At least Portsmouth had fewer marriageable Jewish girls than London; even if he devoted ten minutes to all of them, he'd be through it in under two hours, with plenty of time left to eat and enjoy himself.

But poor Lottie was being dragged through the same ritual in reverse, just a few feet to the southwest, and her sullen murmurs set Elie's teeth on edge. Miss Franchetti's too, he suspected, though they both carried gamely on, swapping anecdotes of farcical letter-writing mix-ups.

"…leaving me no choice," Miss Franchetti said, "but to try to beat the postman to her house and beg him for my letter back—"

"I'm not a *cow*," Lottie said flatly behind him.

Elie and Miss Franchetti both winced. "I really am dying of suspense," he said, "but…"

"No, please, go and rescue Charlotte. She can tell you the end of the story, if you really want to know."

Elie went and tucked his hand into his niece's arm. "I'm going to borrow Lottie for a minute," he told Leah cheerfully. "I hope that's all right."

He led her to the back corner. In his boyhood, the whole cemetery had been about twenty-five feet square, and wasn't large even after a recent purchase of additional land; but the newer section was still mostly empty of congregants either living or dead. Only children would be in earshot if they talked quietly.

Lottie jerked away as soon as he stopped walking. "Issachar Phillips's mother said my full hips would be a great advantage in bearing children!"

Elie grimaced. "Her sister died in childbed and happened to be very thin. But she shouldn't have said that to you."

"She didn't even say it to me. She said it to her son, like I was—"

"—a cow. I heard."

She hunched in on herself. "Sorry I'm not as *agreeable* as you are."

"Enh. Most people aren't, and they do all right for themselves."

She looked surprised, then small and uncertain, as if only her sullenness had been shoring her up.

"Lottie—"

"*Charlotte*," she snapped. "Why won't anybody call me Charlotte?"

"Sorry, I'll try to remember," he said, quashing the urge to protest that she'd never asked. Maybe she had; his memory wasn't perfect. It was almost a comfort, actually, that she would assume he knew—that she never treated him like a stranger, when he'd missed two-thirds of her life. Next week, he would go away again and leave her here.

Not alone, of course—he would leave her in the bosom of her loving family. Was he being foolish again, and deluding himself into feeling indispensable?

But Elie remembered how lonely he had been at sixteen, and for the first time all week, a decision felt simple.

"Charlotte, how are you at keeping secrets? If you'd rather I didn't tell you one, you can say so. It's rather a serious one."

Her eyes lit with curiosity. "I know I used to blurt everything out without thinking when I was younger," she said. "But I can hold my tongue now."

Elie glanced about, making sure even the children had wandered off. "Do you know what a molly is?"

"Yes, it's a man who's like David and Jonathan." Elie must have looked taken aback, because she added, "Because David loved Jonathan 'passing the love of women'—you know. Is that not right? Mamã seemed sure, but she's not always very up-to-date."

Elie felt a little vertiginous. Leah had said that? "No, that's right." He took a deep breath. "Well, I'm one. That's why I've never married."

I3

This didn't get the momentous reaction Elie had expected. Charlotte screwed up her mouth as if trying very hard not to blurt anything out.

Elie had another wave of vertigo. "Does everyone already know?"

"No," Charlotte said hastily. "Not at all. They've wondered about it a few times, that's all. Uncle Morris always says it doesn't matter *why* you don't want to marry, and badgering you won't change your mind." She gave an aggrieved sigh. "But vó's impossible. She says you should marry either way, so you can have children, and anyway people would gossip if she stopped matchmaking."

"Ah." It could have been a lot worse. Even so, Elie decided not to ask what everyone else said. "Please don't tell them I've told you. For now, anyway."

"I won't," she said solemnly.

A memory caught him unawares: Brine sprawled on his bed, saying *On my sacred honor*. He set it aside with a pang. "I told you because—there are also women like that. Who aren't interested in men, and would rather go to bed with women."

Her eyes sparked with interest. "Are there really?"

"Yes. People seem to talk about it less, for some reason. And I just wanted to tell you that if you were like that—if you were like me—it would be all right. You'd be all right." He waited, but she seemed absorbed in her own thoughts. At least she wasn't offended. "I'm not trying to pry," he said at last. "Maybe that's got nothing to do with it. But as your Uncle Morris so wisely said, it doesn't matter *why* you don't want to marry. If you don't want to, you don't have to. And if they go on matchmaking, well…it's their time to waste, I suppose."

Charlotte scowled. "It seems like *my* time to waste."

He laughed. "There is that. Are you afraid of your parents forcing you into anything?" Elie couldn't picture it, himself, but he tried to keep an open mind.

"Not *force* me," she said grudgingly. "But you act as if it's so easy! Maybe it is, for you. They won't leave you alone, and you sit there and listen so politely. But if you get sick of it, you can walk out, and nobody will shout at you even if you stay out all night. You can pack up and get on a coach whenever you like. I live there, and they're my parents, and I *will* live there *until* I marry!"

"That's all very true." He rubbed at his temple. "But it's not as easy as it might look. Especially when it's my mother. Of course I was less independent at sixteen, but I still live with family most of the time, even if it's different branches in different towns. I still work for my uncle. The thing is, Lottie—Charlotte—part of growing up is coming to understand that you *can* say no, and you *can* walk out, and if your parents shout at you over it, you can bear it. It never stops being unpleasant, but sometimes it's that or an arranged marriage."

Her face had retreated back into sullen hardness. "You don't understand."

"Do you want to explain it to me?"

She didn't.

Well, he'd tried. He couldn't help feeling a bit deflated, but the corner of the cemetery was quiet and peaceful, and the wind ruffled his hair pleasantly. Would Aunt Hava be scandalized if he took off his hat? "All right. Maybe I don't understand. Just remember what Hillel said: 'If I am not for myself, who will be for me? If I am only for myself, what am I?'—"

"—And if not now, when?" she finished with an eyeroll. "I suppose we ought to go back."

"Soon is soon enough." Elie leaned against the wall. "I don't think Hillel meant it was now or never. I'm not a scholar, of course, but I always thought he meant…"

"What?"

"Well, that you shouldn't put things off and off. That if something really needs to be done, and you can't start in on it immediately, that you ought to make a plan of some kind."

It all came back to Brine and the accounts, didn't it? He liked to see himself as Charlotte described him: waiting patiently for the wind to pass him by, and then straightening up and going about his business, unmoved. But it wasn't really that easy. You had to be heart of oak, at your center. If you tried to bend and contort yourself to make someone else happy, you just tied yourself in knots. He hadn't been for himself nearly enough with Brine, and now somehow he was angry that Brine hadn't repaid an investment he'd never asked Elie to make, and didn't even know Elie *was* making—just as Brine was indignant that Miss Turner dared to have a mind of her own, after he'd spent thirteen years living like a monk for her sake.

Elie thought of the mess on his desk. Lately he hadn't been for himself enough at Benezet & Sons, either—had taken on everything Uncle Simeon asked him to, when his uncle had certainly never meant for him to take on too much and fall behind. Uncle Simeon hadn't noticed yet, but he would sooner or later. Brine had spotted it at once. He'd said something on one of his very first days home about Elie being under water and needing junior officers to help him bail, and Elie had been charmed by the naval jargon and forgotten all about it.

Elie sighed. He'd wanted to be indispensable, he supposed. But being trustworthy meant answering honestly when Uncle Simeon asked, *Do you have time to…?* They'd have to talk about hiring him an assistant when he was in London next week. But he didn't want just anybody, and when would he have the time to interview applicants? If only there were more hours in the day… If only he'd turned down the *Vliegende Draeck* accounting months ago…

Charlotte broke in on his thoughts. "I might not mind being married someday," she said diffidently, scuffing her toe on the ground. "I don't know. I just know I don't want it *now*. I wish—*you* can travel all over, and make money, and be twenty-six, and nobody ever thinks it's too late for you to get married, and I don't see why I can't do the same—what? What did I say?"

Elie had pushed off the wall, vibrating a little. "You keep the shop's books."

She stared at him. "Yes."

"You're good at it."

"Do you think so?" she asked hopefully. "I don't think I'm *bad* at it, but I do make mistakes sometimes. Last week I added two and six to make nine, and it took me an hour to find where."

"Pfft, everyone does that sometimes. Well—not everyone looks until they find it. Would you like to work for me? I need an assistant rather badly. Especially one who knows Dutch."

"You mean at the counting-house, on the Point?" she said warily.

"It could just be at the counting-house. But if you want to travel with me, I'll talk to your parents."

"You will?" Her eyes were huge. "Wouldn't I—be in your way?"

Elie laughed. "Minha sobrinha, I'd love to have you. What do you imagine I get up to on the road? I just do what I do in Portsmouth, but elsewhere. If you were hoping for a life of incident and adventure, don't take the offer. And I should warn you that the family in London matchmake just as much as yours."

Charlotte's mouth twisted. "Do you really think they can do without me? Who'll keep the books and look after Reuben?"

"They're expecting you to get married soon anyway," he said gently.

"Oh," she said in a small voice. "Right."

He felt sad. "Do you mind if I offer you one more piece of avuncular wisdom?"

She shrugged and looked at her feet.

"I like to feel indispensable too. But the truth is, Charlotte, I'm not. And when I think that I could disappear tomorrow and everyone would just find a way to go on without me, it feels awful. But there's another side of it too, maybe. You all still love me. Meanwhile, I've got clients who rely on me for every little thing, and absolutely despise me. It's good to be useful, but try not to confuse it with being loved. People either love you or they don't. Your family doesn't need you, but they'll *miss* you."

"I think—I'd like to go. Maybe. Probably." She straightened. "I think I would."

"How's this? Nothing's agreed to yet. I'll just suggest the idea to Samuel and Leah, and you can mull it over. I'm going up to town Monday night for a few days. Maybe you could come with me and see how you like it."

She gulped. "And you really think my parents would let me go with you?"

"We won't know until we ask," Elie said, not without inner trepidation. But he didn't regret his offer. (He probably *would*, at least three times a week for the next several years, but hopefully it would be nice the rest of the time.) "I did just tell you I can stand it if people shout at me," he said resignedly. "I didn't expect to have to back my bill quite so soon, but I'm good for it."

Samuel didn't precisely shout, when Elie steeled himself and explained his offer as they waited in line for the mikveh that afternoon. But he said very grimly, "If you let my daughter elope with a sailor, Eleazar, I'm never speaking to you again."

Elie's stomach turned over. Charlotte wouldn't, would she? "Duly noted. But that isn't a refusal."

Samuel glowered. "If we do refuse, Lottie will carry on as if we're blood-soaked despots trampling the fair flower of English liberty. You should have asked me and Leah *before* you spoke to her."

"Probably. I didn't plan it out. She seemed so miserable at the cemetery, and she told me she'd like to work and travel a bit before settling down. Anyway, if she wants to elope with a sailor, she could do it just as easily in Portsmouth. Heaven knows there are enough of them about."

"Yes. I have to admit she's been levelheaded so far, not uniform-mad like some of her friends—wait, she said she wanted to *work*? Lottie? Our Lottie? Every time *we* ask her to do anything besides fuss over those books, she sulks like you wouldn't believe."

"If she's really lazy, then you've nothing to worry about. She'll hate it, and be back at home before Hanukkah."

Samuel's eyes were too bright. "You'll bring her home for Hanukkah regardless." He cleared his throat. "I'll talk to her and Leah. I thought—you know, I thought if she wasn't ready to marry, then I wouldn't have to part with her just yet. It feels like yesterday that she was—" Voice cracking, he held out his hand palm down: *just this tall.*

"I know." Elie sniffled a little himself. "Remember when Brine let her wear his new hat, and we had to stuff it with paper?"

Samuel blew his nose.

"Listen—you know I'd never let her come to any harm if I could possibly prevent it."

"I know." Samuel searched for a clean patch of handkerchief to blot his eyes, and stuffed it back in his pocket. "You'd be such a good father. Are you sure you don't want to let us find you a wife?"

"Quite sure. But thank you."

There was still a light under Brine's door when Elie climbed the stairs after Kol Nidre.

He should have talked to Brine this afternoon, so it would be over and done with.

It wasn't too late to change his mind, and not talk to Brine at all.

But it was astonishing how much clearer everything felt after his conversation with Charlotte. One brief moment of mutual understanding, a single ray of sunlight, and already he breathed easier. He had really only wanted to help Charlotte, because he loved her and she loved him, and it had made everything so simple. It hadn't been like being a pocket calendar, either—but like finally being himself, whole and complete. He had felt that he took up precisely the amount of space his body occupied, no less and no more, and saw things through his own eyes and from his own vantage point, in their proper proportions.

And now, he could no longer avoid seeing where he'd gone wrong, where he'd got tangled up in trying to decipher Miss Turner's cryptic remarks and guess what Brine wanted from him. He'd strained to see himself through their eyes, so he could bend and prune himself to suit their taste.

He'd deluded himself that being useful to Brine could ever satisfy him, when he wanted Brine to love him.

He remembered Brine in the church tower, so dear that Elie's spirit had inclined towards him as surely and instinctively as he'd leaned towards the sea. *Low rations aren't so bad until you smell food,* he'd said.

This would hurt, but surely it would hurt less than keeping Brine forever in view, and cardamom and orange peel forever in his nostrils. It was a new year, and Elie didn't want to waste it.

He knocked. "Brine? Can I talk to you?"

Brine looked very bluff and good-humored when he opened the door, which told Elie he was probably uneasy after yesterday. "Come into my office! How may I assist you?"

Elie sat on the edge of the bed, and couldn't seem to begin.

"Congratulations on your new assistant," Brine said at last. There had been talk of little else at dinner. "You'll have to stop working through meals now. Sixteen-year-olds are always eating."

"Except on Yom Kippur," Elie agreed. "She's already grumbling." He fidgeted with his tzitzit. "I hated Yom Kippur when I was her age too. I used to hide chapbooks inside my siddur. My prayerbook, that is. But nowadays I usually like Kol Nidre. It's, um—"

"When God releases you from your vows. Mrs. Morris explained it to me."

"Yes. Right. But the catch is that HaShem can only absolve you of vows you make to Him. You're still bound by the vows you've made to other people."

"I see," Brine said slowly—plainly not seeing, and plainly expecting criticism of some kind. He was in his striped Guernsey and stocking feet, looking curiously soft and defenseless.

Nausea rose in Elie's throat. "I've been making things very complicated, when they're really very simple: do what you say you'll do, or admit you can't do it and ask to be released."

Brine's brows drew sharply together. "I'm trying," he said. "I'm trying to do what I've promised."

"I know." Elie tried to swallow. "I'm talking about myself. I'm asking you to release me. I'm so sorry. I made you a lot of promises, and— I *will* get you the prize money before the end of your leave, if human ingenuity is equal to it. But I can't be your agent anymore after your marriage." If he vomited after this, HaShem would just have to forgive gargling during the fast.

Brine recoiled. Elie had tried and tried all week to read his face; well, it was easy now. "*What*?"

Somehow, Elie made himself go on. The look on Brine's face might be slicing out his heart, but Brine had been clear, again and again, that his vows to Miss Turner came first. If Elie wasn't for himself, who would be for him? "I'm sorry," he repeated. "But I'm sure Captain Hope's prize agent would be glad to take you on. I should have done this as soon as you were promoted to the wardroom, but I—didn't want to."

Brine went white. "And now you do?"

Elie took a deep breath. "Yes."

Brine's breath came fast and shallow. Elie had expected him to be hurt, but—he hadn't really expected *this*. "Because of how I behaved yesterday?" he said at last, thickly. "I overstepped. I know that. I put you in a bad position. I won't do that again."

I can bear this, Elie told himself. *He's not even shouting.* But he had never felt so guilty in his life. "You aren't to blame," he said. "Please. Please believe me. But I told you yesterday that if I'm your friend as well as your agent, then that was a double reason to exert myself to my utmost in representing your interests. And the truth is, I can't. So I shouldn't represent you."

This week he had finally tasted, almost, what it might be like to be Brine's friend. It had been a revelation, and he'd thought that if it was less than what he wanted, it might still be enough. But next week, Miss Turner would be Brine's wife.

And probably sooner or later, in the hustle and bustle of career and family, Elie would be only his agent again.

He'd tried and tried to believe Brine's marriage wouldn't matter—that she would be far away—that he could still write to Brine—that he wouldn't mind running her errands and furnishing her house and buying her baby clothes. But it would matter, and he would mind, actually. He hated the idea.

Brine shook his head. "I know you. You'd never cheat me."

"No. But there are degrees of temptation, as you told me yourself, not too long ago." If Brine asked him what the hell he was talking about, Elie could not possibly produce an innocent explanation.

But Brine didn't, actually, look confused anymore. He stared at Elie, and took a step closer, as if he couldn't help himself. "And what are you tempted to do?"

Suddenly Elie was hot and breathless, his thoughts winking out one by one like stars at daybreak. In another minute, he might do anything. In desperation, he said tartly, "Miss Turner asked me if I really believed you wanted to marry her, and I was strongly tempted to tell her no."

Brine fell back with a gasp.

"That's what I thought," Elie said. "Don't worry, I didn't do it."

There was silence. Brine looked rather as if he were drowning.

Elie stood up. "I'll finish the prize accounting for you. I'll compensate you however you like, for giving you so little notice." He hesitated. "Brine, if you ever really *need* my assistance…or if my connections can be of use to you…"

Brine's jaw dropped. "You can't be serious. You think I'd ask you for *patronage*?"

"You must suit yourself, of course," Elie said, falling back on professional formulae. "But why shouldn't you? I didn't mean to—I don't want to part on bad terms."

"Why shouldn't I?" Brine repeated slowly. "Next you'll offer to forgive my debt."

"Gladly, if you—"

Brine's laugh was like the crack of a lash. "Oh no, I'm not an investment to you," he said with indescribable bitterness. "I'd have to be worth something for that."

"You know that's not what I meant!"

"No, of course it isn't. I'm sure you meant something extremely fine indeed. You and Sarah both—you're very free with pretty abstractions, but when I convert them to cold, hard facts, they seem to add up to you writing off your association with me as a bad debt, so you can invest in a more promising venture. While I sunk everything I had!" His voice rose sharply, and broke.

"You're the one getting back on a ship next week." *You're the one getting married.* Elie had never expected heartbreak to feel this spiteful. "I'm sorry," he said with an effort. "That was—"

"Unprofessional?" Brine bit out.

Elie flushed hot. He *had* almost used that word, as ludicrous as it was. "Unfair. Dishonest."

I will stake my honor on his probity.

The flush faded, leaving him cold and clear-eyed. He knew what needed to be done: give up his pride, admit his transgression, and ask to make amends. He'd always known that; he only hadn't *done* it.

The worst of it was, this squirming resistance in his chest was familiar. Every year between Rosh Hashanah and Yom

Kippur, he contemplated difficult apologies and decided it was better not to. *Mãe's already forgotten all about that,* he'd tell himself, and *That insufferable receiver at the Deptford warehouse will only gloat if I apologize for being sharp with him.*

Elie cast his mind back to the afternoon, to his moment of clarity and mutual understanding with Charlotte. Even setting aside what he owed Brine, didn't he deserve some peace, himself?

"I've sunk more in you than you know," he said at last. "I never wanted you to know. I lied to you about it. I told myself I didn't expect a return, and then I resented you when I didn't get one. That isn't good business *or* friendship. *That's* why I'm resigning as your agent, Brine."

"What are you talking about?"

"I've been taking a loss on you." There. He'd said it. Elie felt rather as if he had snow blindness. "Systematically. I paid a guinea for that sextant I sold you for eighteen shillings. I knew you wouldn't let me do it if I asked you, and I did it anyway. I'm deeply sorry. I hope you can forgive me."

14

There was a long, disorienting silence. Elie had hoped maybe he would feel better when it was out. He emphatically did not.

Brine's expression had been wiped clean with shock. At last he leaned back against the wall. Reflexively, Elie noted the alluring line of his shoulders. "And I suppose if I don't forgive you, I can file a lawsuit?" Then he shook his head. "No. No, you can't tell me that was business. Was it charity?"

"Of course not. Charity is giving to the Widow and Orphans fund. Brine—I—" Elie quailed. "I had the money, and you didn't. It seemed fair to go snacks. Maybe there'd *be* fewer widows and orphans, if—"

"You're telling me it was *patriotism*?"

Elie turned his hands palm up, helplessly. "I liked you, obviously." That was less than the truth, and far too much for safety. But they had left safety behind a long time ago. "I didn't want you to go without. That's all."

"How many of your clients have you done this for?"

"One."

"Christ…" Brine passed a hand over his face. "Do you know how much it was? Can I pay it back?"

"I'd much rather you didn't. But if you decide you have to, then yes, I can tell you how much it was."

"How many people *know* about this?"

"Only Samuel and Morris, as far as I know. I didn't tell them. They just noticed, over the years." He sighed. "Probably the whole house knows. I'm so sorry. It got out of my control."

Brine bowed his head, pressing his forehead into his steepled index fingers. "Degrees of temptation…" he muttered. "It has to stop dead once my prize money comes in, do you understand?"

Everything would stop dead when the prize money came in. But Elie couldn't suppress a flash of startled wonder that Brine hadn't said *from today.* He hadn't asked for a figure.

Brine slumped at the edge of the bed like a puppet with cut strings. "You know the Wednesday toast. 'Ourselves, as no-one else is likely to concern themselves with our welfare.'"

"Yes."

"You feel—marooned, sometimes, at sea. Cast out and forgotten. I wrote to you a lot in those early days, didn't I? I forwarded you every penny I could scrape together." He huffed a defeated little laugh. "To pay my debts."

Elie nodded.

"It wasn't only financial integrity." Brine's mouth twisted. "I wanted to remind you of my existence. I liked thinking that somewhere, you were concerning yourself with my welfare."

"I was." Elie's voice was a thread.

"It's humiliating, and it's sneaking, what you did." Brine kept his gaze fixed on his own hand, lying on the bed. Elie remembered sitting in just that spot to bandage Brine's foot, and the way Brine had tugged at his dressing-gown button. He'd never look at Elie like that again. Maybe he'd never look at Elie again, at all. "And I'm base enough to be glad of it anyway. I've never been heart of oak." His hand fisted in the coverlet. "You should go. Before I forfeit any more self-respect."

MONDAY
YOM KIPPUR
"Our ships at sea."

No amount of davening or fidgeting with his fringes could soothe Elie at synagogue the next day.

It has to stop dead once my prize money comes in. Last night he'd taken that as some kind of—blessing, almost, when he should have understood it for the condemnation it was. Brine had despised himself for wanting to keep Elie's money, when he couldn't pay it back regardless. He couldn't make a clean break with Elie if he wanted to. Not until his prize money came in and made him independent.

And Elie had procrastinated the prize accounting. *That,* Brine still didn't know. An image of the defeated slump of Brine's beautiful wide shoulders pierced Elie's heart again.

"Sit still!" Samuel elbowed him. "You're as bad as the kids."

"Stop exaggerating." Gracia was currently on the floor tying and untying the laces of Elie's cloth shoes, Zach was openly staring at the ceiling, Aaron was napping under his father's talet, and Hyam and Kaatje had wandered off and were running around the back of the synagogue with their cousins and friends. Elie couldn't pick out Reuben from the polyphony of crying babies, but Morris's anxious glances at the women's gallery suggested his voice was among them.

Elie beat his breast a little harder than necessary as he recited Ashamnu—soothed a little after all by the solid thump of knuckles on bone. The prayer was a broad catalog of sins in alphabetical order, so no misdeed might be forgotten or glossed over. Among the preprinted list, some stood out, reverberating in Elie's chest with peculiar, personal force: *We have been presumptuous. We have lied. We have been corrupt in our dealings.*

Elie had known HaShem hated unequal weights and unequal measures, and he'd pretended it was all right because he had his hand on the scale in Brine's favor and not his own. Either you did what you said you would, or you got in the habit of prevaricating and then somehow you were late paying out twelve hundred pounds when your client really needed it.

He'd apologized to Brine, but what was an apology without amends?

On Rosh Hashanah it is written, the congregation chanted, *and on Yom Kippur it is sealed…* Only a few more hours to convince the Almighty it was worth advancing Elie another year—that He could trust Elie to make something of it, this time.

What did Elie want to make of it?

Well—he wanted a clean heart, and a steadfast spirit. He wanted to be trustworthy, and live in accordance with his own principles. He wanted to set a good example for Charlotte, who would model her professional conduct on his. He wanted a lot of other things too—complicated, impossible things. But this was simple, and it was within his reach.

Elie was tired of procrastination and excuses. If there was ever a day to say *Now or never,* surely it was Yom Kippur.

Reuben was wailing loud enough now to be unmistakable. Then his shrieks grew fainter and descended; evidently he was being carried down the stairs. Morris stood.

"I'll check on them for you, if you like," Elie said.

"Such altruism," Morris said, but he let Elie go.

When Elie came into the foyer, it was Charlotte rocking the red-faced baby. She broke off singing to cough. "I'm so thirsty! Only another thirty-six hours or so until sunset."

Elie glanced around nearly as fearfully as he had before admitting to being a molly. "What would you say to telling everyone the baby won't calm down, and going home? We can take Gracia and Aaron too—Aaron's going to wake up any minute and fuss. The truth is, I could use your help with some work. I know we shouldn't, but—I think I've got to finish Mr. Brine's prize accounting before the gates close."

Her eyes lit up. "*Please.*"

Patty (though a Gentile and working on the holiday herself) was mildly scandalized. But she lit a fire and the lamps in the first-floor parlor, and sent a boy to the counting-house for the crate of *Vliegende Draeck* papers.

HaShem would close His gates at sunset. Elie's pocket calendar informed him that would be 5:35 p.m. today—5:40 in Portsmouth, thank goodness. By two, he was feeling hopeful, and let Charlotte begin searching the Prize List for the names of recent deserters while he tried to lull Reuben back to sleep. She had been even more of a help than he'd expected, and over and above her good grounding in bookkeeping by double-entry, had a gift for deciphering bad handwriting.

Then he heard Brine's step on the stair. The door opened.

It was a cloudy day, promising rain. Brine was dim and brown as a Rembrandt in the shadowed doorway, catching the light only here and there: an earlobe, the whites of his eyes, the flat of his nose, the curving upper planes of chin and lips and broken cheekbone. It wasn't *fair*.

"Mr. Eleazar? What are you doing at home?" His eyes fell on the papers spread over the carpet. "Tell me you're not shirking synagogue in favor of drudgery on an empty stomach."

"Reuben wouldn't stop crying." Elie squirmed a little. "And I have to finish the *Draeck* accounting."

Did the color drain from Brine's face? A trick of the light, maybe. But he swayed on his feet and caught the door jamb.

Elie started forward. "Are you ill?" he said sharply. Little Reuben's eyes flew wide open. "No, Ru-ru, shshsh, it's all right."

Charlotte was already on her feet, taking the baby. "Mr. Brine?"

Brine smiled reassuringly at her. "I had a penny glass of gin, that's all. Just one. Nothing to worry about." But his gaze returned to the papers almost at once, smile fading. "Can you really not wait to see the back of me?"

By now even Gracia and Aaron had stopped playing to watch the unfolding drama.

"Let's talk upstairs." Elie rang for Patty to help with the children, and then sent Brine up the stairs ahead of him, in case he stumbled.

But he seemed steady on his feet now. He pulled Elie into his room and shut the door with no trace of clumsiness. He was so close. Even when Elie retreated until his hat-brim hit the door, Brine was *right there*, smelling very faintly of gin and more strongly of orange peel and cardamom, and Elie was so hungry that for a second, *he* swayed on his feet.

"You've got to stop," Brine said fiercely.

"In Heaven's name, *why*? Isn't this what you wanted?"

"What I *wanted*?" Brine echoed. "God!" His breath came short and fast through his nostrils. He took Elie's hand in a tight, convulsive grip. "Put off the distribution another few days. Just until I'm at sea again. Please."

<h1 style="text-align:center">15</h1>

lie might actually faint. Brine just *had* to do this on a fast day, didn't he? "So you don't want to marry Miss Turner after all?"

"I wish I could." Brine's voice rasped in his throat. "But I can't. I've tried and tried to bend myself to it, and I—*can't.*"

Elie put his free hand over Brine's. "Then don't," he said gently. "It's like you said, remember? We can't always bend like the reed, for we have hearts of oak."

"Don't." Brine jerked away. "Don't try to turn it into something noble. You told me yourself: even God can't release me from the vow I made to her."

"No, but she can."

"I *owe* her," Brine said in despair. "But that's just the trouble, isn't it? She said it herself—that I had left you the keepsakes and her the money, and didn't I think that was backwards? I—ahem. I meant to tell you I updated my will. I left you my watch in it."

"I know, I listened to your conversation in the pantry," Elie said, to work his way up to the larger confession.

Brine groaned. "I hoped against hope you had been too conscientious."

Elie could see him begin to go back over the conversation, wincing at the most offensive parts. "Don't apologize. I haven't been conscientious, Brine. I tried to tell you that, but I couldn't bring myself—I didn't know how—" He spit it out at last. "I was already putting off the distribution."

Brine went still.

"That's why I was determined to finish today. Because I've been putting it off for months, in one way or another, and it was wrong of me. In my defense, I didn't know you and Miss Turner would be here until you *were* here, but—"

"You were putting it off." He didn't appear to be breathing.

"The statute only says 'within a reasonable period of time'—" Elie began halfheartedly. "Yes. I couldn't bring myself to start."

"Why?" Brine demanded. That was hope in his face, wasn't it? "Because you knew how *I* felt, or because—"

"I still don't know how you feel."

"Not how I should." Brine's eyes seared into him. He shifted closer—to see if Elie tried to retreat? Elie couldn't have moved if he tried. "I was your client and I hated it when you treated me like one, because I wanted to be…friends. And all the while Sarah is—*was* going to be my wife, and all I want is to square accounts with her. I thought it would be all right. But yesterday when you were ramming your patronage down my throat—" He faltered. "Both of you tried to tell me, that she doesn't want my money or my duty. She wants what you've been giving me all these years—she wants deeds of loving kindness. I saw the difference so clearly last night, when you'd gone. And I can't give that to her. It's not in me." He squared his shoulders. Elie felt his tension, but his eyes never wavered, and his hand didn't shake as he laid it flat on the door by Elie's ear. "I never paid attention to whether *she* was eating her dinner."

Elie's heart turned over in his chest. *Mr. Brine showed great coolness and decision...* "I, er—" He searched for a balance between acting in Brine's interests and acting in his own. "Is it necessary for your peace of mind to resolve the question of Miss Turner before moving to another subject?"

The corner of Brine's mouth curved up unexpectedly. "Mm," he said in a way that might have meant *yes,* or might not have. "Better get out your pocket calendar." His hand curled around Elie's waist, suddenly, sliding down his coat-tail and delving into his hip pocket.

"I'm not sure— I don't wish to repeat— She's rather cryptic," Elie stammered as Brine slid out his calendar. "But I'm not sure she has any great expectation of marrying you anyway."

"No?" Brine tilted his head with an arrested expression, Elie's calendar held lightly in his right palm. "Hunh. She certainly isn't in a hurry." He ran his left thumb along the edge as if to open it.

Elie's pulse raced. "You've got it upside—"

Brine pinched the little book between finger and thumb, and tossed it over his shoulder onto the bed. "That's better," he said, eyes gleaming. "I've been wanting to do that all week."

Elie could not possibly be imagining things. If Brine's hand had slid just a few inches lower, it would have been cupping his arse. He could flirt, and let on that he meant it. He could *be here,* with Brine.

He relaxed against the door, and smiled. A racing pulse was pleasant when you didn't have to hide it—warm and a little intoxicating. "You've been wanting to throw my things onto your bed all week?"

Brine broke out into a dazzling, relieved grin. "Not quite. Now, where were we? Ah, yes…" He put a hand back on the door, curling the other around Elie's waist, and when Elie leaned into his palm, his smile spread to reveal the edge of his crooked teeth. "What was it your Mr. Hillel said? 'If you'd hate it, don't do it to the other fellow'?"

"Close enough." But it wasn't close enough. He drew Brine in until he smelled cardamom and orange, closing his eyes to revel in Brine's roughened jaw brushing his, and the soft, worn texture of Brine's lapels under his palms. Brine's hair tickled his temple and unbalanced his hat.

"Mr. Eleazar?" Brine's voice in his ear was low and intimate.

"Call me Elie."

And Brine did. His name had never sounded like that in anyone else's mouth, yielding as a ripe plum.

"I wouldn't hate it," Brine said, "if you did it to me."

Elie broke his fast.

Someone knocked on the door. Elie started violently. His hat would certainly have fallen off, if it hadn't already joined his calendar on Brine's bed several minutes ago.

"Uncle Elie?" Charlotte said tentatively in the corridor. "I've finished with the Prize List. What's next?"

"Actually…" He cleared his throat and tried, mostly unsuccessfully, to stop thinking about Brine's thigh between his legs. "I'm very sorry, Charlotte, but circumstances have changed. We needn't finish by sunset. Oh, and we won't go up to London tonight. But I'll take you up for Dividend Day and— I'll be down in a moment."

Brine snickered. "You don't think that's a trifle optimistic?" Elie put a hand over his mouth. Brine licked his palm.

"You can't be serious," Charlotte said. "Next you'll want to go back to synagogue!"

"Probably," Elie admitted. "Sorry. Seems like bad luck not to, and I enjoy the reading of Jonah."

There was a pause. "*Good* changed circumstances? Is everyone all right, I mean?"

Brine pushed Elie's hand away. "Everyone's fine, Miss Lazarus. I'm not getting married this week, that's all."

His fingers stayed lightly curled around Elie's wrist. The inside of a wrist was more sensitive than Elie had fully appreciated. He wanted to put his mouth on Brine's pulse. He wanted to find patches of Brine's skin that even the sun hadn't marked, and bite him there.

Brine would let him. Brine, Elie felt confident, would like it.

"Oh," Charlotte said, a world of curiosity in her voice.

"Minha sobrinha, I love you, but go away. I'll be there— soon."

Silence had fallen. Brine was gazing dreamily at the ceiling, his brow smooth and untroubled, his mouth curving just a little.

"Listen," Elie said, extremely reluctantly. "About Miss Turner."

Brine sat up, brow contracting, and Elie felt a sudden tenderness for the kid he'd once been, who'd kissed a girl and thought finally everything would be plain sailing.

"Forgive me," Elie said, "but I'd rather not delay the accounting on purpose to deceive her. A humane loophole is all well and good; abuse of trust is something else. Please don't believe that I'll think any of the less of *you*, for behaving towards her however you think safe, and right. But for myself… I'd rather not."

"No," Brine said. "I shouldn't have asked you to."

"You can ask me for anything. I'll give you what I can."

"Heart of oak." Brine smiled crookedly. "I suppose I'd better ask her to release me. I've been turning over what you said about praying for me to live through the year. I never think so far ahead. I think I've been—expecting to die young, and jury-rigging my life as if it only had to make it into port. I was glad to marry Sarah, if it meant she'd have rights as my widow. And then I thought about retiring and spending my old age with her, and—well—" He covered his eyes with one hand, and confessed, "My first thought was to hope I wouldn't live that long. Poor Sarah! When she's such a darling."

Elie, who wouldn't have chosen the word *darling* to describe Miss Turner, was a little startled. He thought she might have been startled by it too. "What would you build," he asked, "if you were building to last?"

Brine's smile broke out again. "I would make me a willow cabin at your gate, and call upon my soul within the house…" Here he became distracted by kissing Elie's fingers—sucking the thumb into his mouth to the first knuckle, then releasing it with an indecent little smacking sound to press an open-mouthed kiss to Elie's palm.

"That doesn't sound very sturdy," said Elie, still a little confounded by Brine's desire.

"You'd have to let me inside when it rained," Brine said, making it sound very filthy indeed.

"But then," Elie remarked to himself, "even *The Seaman's Guide and Coaster's Companion* would sound filthy if you read it in that tone of voice."

"Don't remind me! *You* could read *The Seaman's Guide* in any tone of voice and it would be filthy. Thank God I was dead drunk, or I'd have made an ass of myself—but of course if I hadn't been dead drunk, I'd never have suggested it. At least I didn't let you read in Portuguese." His eyes darkened. "Come here." He pulled Elie into his lap, then—evidently still unsatisfied—maneuvered until he was flat on his back with Elie draped over him like a blanket. "I don't have to behave myself anymore," he said. "God, what a joke! I've behaved disgracefully all week. But I didn't put my hands on you. Much." He hooked one leg around Elie's. "When you come to me tonight, bring the lamp, and do up all the buttons on that dressing gown. I mean to open them with my teeth."

Elie considered a joke about outranking Brine, and kissed his broken cheekbone instead. "Do you remember when we climbed the church tower?"

"Vividly. The light was spectacular and there was no one else about. I could scarcely look at you. Thank God those tinted glasses gave me an excuse to stare at the sea instead."

"But you always stare at the sea," Elie said stupidly. "No, wait, I meant to tell you something. It's very difficult to think when you— Oh, yes. You asked me what I don't think about."

Brine didn't move, exactly, but Elie felt something in him thrum, like one magnet drawn to another. "Tell me. Please."

"You," Elie said. Brine's hands tightened on his waist. "I don't think about you. I don't think about you all the time." His lips twitched. "I don't think about you when I lie down or when I rise up, when I sit at home or—"

"You can read me Deuteronomy in a filthy tone of voice later," Brine said, a little unsteadily. "Will you forgive me, Elie? For handling everything so badly, and keeping you and Sarah both waiting so long, for nothing?"

"Pfft, I'd already forgotten all about that! Er—sorry. My mouth runs away with me sometimes. You've probably noticed, but it's much worse when I'm happy. Yes, I forgive you. With all my heart. Thanks for asking."

Brine gave rather a formal little nod, and then he smirked and said wickedly, "How can I make it up to you?"

Elie shifted, laying his cheek on Brine's chest. He could hear Brine's heartbeat, an everyday miracle. "I can think of so many things I want from you. I want you to let me take care of you, and I want you to meet my mother, and I want to introduce you to my uncle and his influential friends so you can be master attendant at Sheerness one day. Which reminds me, I want rather badly to ram my patronage down your throat. If you take my meaning. I'd also quite like you to bend me over my desk."

He could feel Brine open his mouth to speak.

"But most of all," Elie said, "I want you to arrange your life so that you wish more than anything to keep living it. I'd prefer it was with me, obviously. But only if that makes you happy."

Brine's chest rose and fell unevenly. "I believe— I can promise you that. I'll have to think about some of the rest of it." His fingers were shy in Elie's hair. "Do you think your mother will like me?"

"Yes. But if she doesn't, it won't be the end of the world."

"All that means you'll be my agent again, doesn't it? If I must have a prize agent, then I must, but I'd rather have you."

"Yes," Elie said. "If you're sure."

Brine tipped Elie's chin up, to look him in the eye. "I wouldn't—I wouldn't really object to letting you—take care of me," he said haltingly. Pink was spreading across his cheekbones. "But if I take your money and let you do me favors, won't you think less of me, by and by? A man shouldn't sponge on his friends."

"Ai, anjo meu!" Elie said, a little incredulously, and kissed his fingers. "Men sponge on their friends all the time. It's not your fault the Navy doesn't pay you enough to live on. Would it seem more natural if you thought of it—of me— not as a friend, but as…?" Why was this the most difficult thing of all to say? "As family," he mumbled into Brine's waistcoat.

Brine didn't hear. "Pardon?"

"As family!"

"Oh," Brine said. "Oh. I—do you mean that?"

It was borne in upon him that family was another commodity of which he had a superabundance, and Brine had a deficit. "I'd like it very much." He thought of Brine's will: his hat for Charlotte, odds and ends for the other little Lazaruses. He propped himself up on his forearms. "And I'm sure if you asked the children to call you uncle, they'd be thrilled. If you wished to, that is."

Brine glowed. He opened and closed his mouth a few times, then evidently decided this was too much good fortune to look full in the face. "You really think I could get a dockyard? You don't think it's flying too high?"

"I think it's possible, and I think you'd run it splendidly if you did," Elie said. "Of course it's not a sure thing. Brilliant masters outnumber dockyards. But there are plenty of lesser positions to fall back on."

"By then you'll be a partner in Benezet & Sons and have the Navy Board's ear," Brine said with fond pride, "and I'll be obliged to wear my dress uniform when I go about with you, to uphold your dignity."

Elie kissed him, hard. "I don't want you to go away next week. I'll miss you immoderately. Send word next time you resupply at Yarmouth, so I can manufacture an errand there."

"I'll count the days," Brine promised. "Maybe I could drill holes in our water butts, to hurry things along." He bit his lip. "You're sure you won't get tired of waiting for me?"

"I think I shall like waiting for you," Elie admitted. "Of course it would be nicer to have you at home, but I—well, I do travel a great deal myself. And I was just thinking last week what charming love letters you would write, and how I'd like to keep them in their own pigeonhole tied up with ribbon and reread them on difficult days."

Brine drew in a sharp breath.

"That is," Elie added, suddenly self-conscious, "I do already give your letters their own pigeonhole and reread them on difficult days. But I expect it will have a more cheering effect now. And who knows, the war may even end someday—"

Brine gave an odd bark of laughter, and nudged Elie aside so he could rise and dig for something in his trunk. "Don't laugh at me."

"You're the one who just—"

Brine thrust a bundle into his lap, tied up with twine. He tugged the slip-knot free, and watched Elie.

Elie unwrapped the oilcloth. Inside were his own letters. In fact, Elie—who numbered his envelopes for each client so they'd know if any were lost in the post—could see that it was nearly all three hundred and twelve of them.

"It's only good recordkeeping to save your agent's letters." Brine was coiling the twine round his finger, as if by habit. It had been repurposed from another parcel; old knots and sealing wax dangled. "That's what I planned to tell anyone who remarked on it, anyway."

A cracked wafer caught the light: a storm-tossed ship under the motto *SUCH IS LIFE.* Elie blinked. "Is that—my seal?"

Brine raised his eyebrows.

"Well, that design is hardly particular to me, I've sold dozens of them myself—"

"That method of tying up a parcel is particular to you," he retorted. "You use two figure-of-eight loops to pull it snug."

"I do, don't I," Elie said faintly. "It only works with good twine; otherwise you snap it."

Brine's brows drew together. "I told myself I must be making it up." He sounded almost accusing. "I told myself I didn't know you very well, and that thinking about you was only a way of passing time on blockade, and probably if I did get to know you, you'd be altogether different than I imagined."

"And am I?"

He sighed. "Oh, yes. You're better. It's very provoking of you."

"People in glass houses!" Downstairs, Reuben started to cry. Elie winced. "I've abandoned Charlotte and Patty *much* too long."

"Of course." Brine wrapped the letters carefully up again. "Go. I'd better find Sarah."

"Good luck."

"Thanks." He felt under the bed for the pocket calendar and blew the dust off it. Elie reached out, but Brine opened it. The reversed binding did baffle him briefly, but he fished his reading glasses and a pencil from his pocket and flipped through, scribbling something before handing it over.

There was a note beside today's date, in small, neat letters:

late p.m., private conference with
Mr. A. Brine of HMS Steadfast.

N.B.— bring: { *(i) buttons;*
(ii) lamp.

Epilogue

The evening sky was still streaked with crimson when Elie finally left synagogue with his family—even Charlotte, who had decided nursemaiding on her own was more trouble than it was worth. Despite his ravenous appetite, he left the Lazarus family on their doorstep and continued down Queen Street, just to where the harbor came into view between the shops and the dockyard wall.

The water was scarlet and orange and deep green, the hulls of the farthest ships indistinguishable below the pale smears of their sails. *Red sky at night, sailor's delight.*

Was it only last week that Elie had thought that sunset was like winter coming on, an end to the day's hopes? And yet Jewish holy days began at sundown; HaShem had created the world at evening. Elie should have known better. This sunset was the beginning of a new day, a new year, a new life. Night was full of possibilities—*tonight* was full of possibilities. *Blessed are You, who makes the evening fall.*

He thought he could pick out the *Steadfast*, but he wished Brine were here to confirm it. He hurried home, hoping Brine would be there—but even if he wasn't, he would be later. He'd made a firm appointment.

As it turned out, Brine was arguing with Miss Turner in the pantry again. Elie was tempted to leave them there—the smell of dinner was a siren song—but instead he apologized to

Patty and shooed them into the passageway. "Now, if you'll excuse me—"

Brine threw him a pleading look. "I'm very sorry, Mr. Eleazar, we'll let you get to your dinner as soon as possible. But I've tried laying it all out for her as you did the other day, how we might settle matters, and she—"

"I don't need your money, Augie, honestly."

"Maybe if you explained it to her—"

"No, Mr. Eleazar, you explain to this lump of—"

"This is between you," Elie broke in. "And Brine, I represent you, so it's a conflict of interest for me to advise Miss Turner on this matter."

Miss Turner smiled upon him. "You do not disappoint me, Mr. Eleazar. I am so glad to leave Augie in good hands."

Brine blushed. "I wish you'd let me give you the money, Sarah," he said doggedly, "after I've led you such a dance."

"Oh, pooh," she said. "I *was* disappointed when I realized it would never come to anything, but that was years ago now, and really I think it's for the best. For myself as well, I mean."

"I always meant to keep my word," Brine said despairingly.

She patted him on the shoulder. "I'm quite sure you did." She looked at his woebegone face. "Oh dear, I suppose I shall have to tell you. Mr. Eleazar, you can witness that I've released Mr. Brine from his promise at his own request. Isn't that so, Augie?"

"Yes, but—"

"Perhaps I'd better get it in writing," she said, so that was a fresh delay as Elie ran upstairs for his lapdesk. "I don't need your money," she repeated when the hastily drafted statement was duly signed. "I'm rich."

The only sound for a few moments was the growling of Elie's stomach. "That's absurd," Brine said.

"You're absurd," she said tartly. "I, on the other hand, am the manufacturer of All Hands On Deck."

"Oh." Elie's eyes widened as the myriad implications of this sank in. "So *that's* why you were asking me about contracts."

"Yes. I *could* be richer, I think," she said. "I don't believe my arrangement with Mr. Doggett is really to my advantage. I hope you will advise me, Mr. Eleazar. As it's nothing to do with Mr. Brine any longer, there can be no conflict of interest, surely."

"I should be delighted," said Elie in a daze. "If Mr. Brine has no objection."

She beamed. "I would have asked you originally, instead of Mr. Doggett, except…er…"

"Except you didn't want *me* to know, I suppose," Brine finished for her, looking hurt. "Why not?"

Miss Turner coughed apologetically. "Well, you see, Augie," she said, "I thought if you knew I was making money, you might actually want to marry me."

"But I offered to release you, and you refused!"

"I thought being engaged might make things safer for you," she said. "It's not as though I were planning to marry someone else, so it didn't put *me* out. I'm sure I never meant to get in your way. Sailors are popularly supposed to have a highly pragmatic notion of fidelity—'wives and sweethearts, may they never meet,' et cetera."

Brine was speechless.

Even Elie hadn't dreamed that the matter would work itself out quite so neatly. But he tried not to sound too giddy; he didn't want Miss Turner to think he was gloating. "In short, you're very fond of one another and have both been doing your best to be helpful, despite not knowing each other very well at all. Now it's a new year, and you can start afresh. Why don't you both come and have dinner?" But he made for the dining room without waiting for their answer.

His family at once began clamoring to fill his plate. "Try the beef, it's very tender."

"Here's the tzimmes—take all the apricots, no one else cares for them."

"He's a grown man, he can make up his own plate," said Morris, passing him the rolls.

Charlotte laughed and slid his favorite chutney towards him.

"Yes, Mr. Eleazar, better keep your strength up," Brine said wickedly as he passed behind Elie's chair.

"Ah, there you are, Mr. Brine." Aunt Hava filled his glass. "Have some salmagundi… Oh, more lettuce than that! Sailors never get enough fresh food."

"I shouldn't like to take more than my share, ma'am."

"Don't be silly, vó bought it for you." Charlotte raised her wine. "To our ships at sea!"

Brine toasted her, glowing brighter than the candles. "To friends at home," he proposed.

"To a sweet new year," Elie said, and thought it would be.

Author's Note

Thank you for reading "Sailor's Delight"! I hope you enjoyed Elie and Augie's story.

Would you like to know when my next book is available? Sign up for updates at RoseLerner.com or follow me on Twitter at @RoseLerner. You can also support me on Patreon, for weekly sneak peeks at what I'm working on. (My Patreon patrons also named the *Steadfast* and chose Augie's signature scent, among other vital contributions!)

Reviews help other readers find books. I appreciate all reviews, positive and negative.

If you'd like to see Elie's first cameo in my books and find out what happened with his friend Jael in Rye Bay, check out *The Wife in the Attic*. It's a sapphic Jane Eyre retelling, in which the governess falls for the…well, it's right there in the name. *Wife* is also available as an Audible Original audiobook.

Fair warning: *Wife* is a Gothic, and quite a bit darker than this story! If that's not your speed, don't worry—my other historical romances are closer to this one in tone. If you're not sure where to start, try "All or Nothing," in which a shy architect asks a gaming den hostess to pose as his mistress so he can get work done during his ex-boyfriend's scandalous house party, or *Sweet Disorder*, in which a wounded army officer matchmakes for a prickly widow to help his brother win a local election.

Visit my website for "Sailor's Delight" extras, including historical research and deleted scenes.

Turn the page to learn more about my other romances.

THE WIFE IN THE *Attic*

GOLDENGROVE'S TOWERS rose at the very edge of the peaceful Weald, a stone's throw from the poisonous marshes and merciless waters of Rye Bay. Young Tabby Palethorp had been running wild there ever since her mother grew too ill to leave her room.

I was the perfect governess: thoroughly respectable and far too plain to tempt Tabby's lonely father, Sir Kit, to indiscretion.

I knew better than to trust my new employer with the truth about my past. But knowing better couldn't stop me from yearning for impossible things: to be Tabby's mother, Sir Kit's companion, Goldengrove's mistress.

All that belonged to poor Lady Palethorp. Most of all, I burned to finally catch a glimpse of her. Surely *she* could tell me why all the doors inside the house were locked after dark, and whose footsteps I heard in the night…

"It gave me nightmares…a furious, tender, aching, incisive masterpiece of a book." —Olivia Waite, author of *The Lady's Guide to Celestial Mechanics*

Chapter 1

Already I couldn't get any air. I knew it would be better to breathe in the smoke and suffocate before the fire reached my toes, but I couldn't. I lacked the strength even to turn my head away as heat kissed my face and the flames licked closer, closer…

I bolted upright, drenched in sweat, my heart pounding and the sheets tangled around my legs. I checked the bedside table and the hearth, but no candle burned, no coal smoldered. Only a few rays of pale moonlight lit my drab little room; no shade of red or yellow intruded.

It was barely three o'clock, with no chance of breakfast until half past eight, but I knew from long experience I wouldn't sleep again. I would be bone-tired all day, and it served me right for putting the extra blanket on the bed. I knew better, but I'd been so sick of shivering through the night, feeling the cold seep through my skin to the core of me.

It was too early to practice my guitar without waking Mrs. Humphrey's other boarders, and any other employment would require light. I couldn't bring myself to use my tinderbox. A candle would be all right once it was lit, a small friendly flame safely housed in Papa's old mica sea lantern, but striking the uncontrolled sparks…

In an hour, I promised myself. In an hour I would forget the nightmare, light the damn candle, and read *The Miseries of an Heiress.*

It would be a relief to immerse myself in miseries so entirely removed from mine. My own father, though his pension had supported us while he lived, had left me barely enough to pay for his funeral and a few new words on my mother's old stone. That out of the way, my inheritance came to: the lantern; Papa's second-best wooden leg, currently serving as a hatstand; mãe's guitar, a plain but sturdy instrument I kept for my students to learn upon; and a handful of odds and ends.

I never lit the candle. I had bought foul-smelling lard candles that week, anyway, not having the extra penny for the tallow we had always used at home. I lay in my bed watching dawn creep across the warped boards in the ceiling, and at a quarter past eight dressed in a hurry and went down to the dining-room. I could immediately smell that the porridge was burnt.

Breakfast at Mrs. Humphrey's had never been plentiful or well-seasoned, but these last few months were a new nadir. We'd lost our maid-of-all-work, Sukey, just before Christmas, and I missed her heartily. Since then we'd been through six servants, and I felt certain the newest one would burn the house to the ground one fine day.

Of course Mrs. Humphrey didn't mind. When the porridge was scorched, we ate less of it.

Iphigenia Lemmon pushed her spice-box towards me. I took as much of her salt as conscience would allow, and together we choked the oatmeal down. Some days, this ritual amused me. Today, I saw a thousand such mornings stretched out ahead of me, thin and gray and unappetizing.

The maid-of-all-work in question brought in a folded note. Beside me, Miss Starling's fingers tightened on her spoon as though she might leap up from the table and stab the girl with it.

The note was held out to *me*. "What answer shall I give Lady Tassell's footman, ma'am? He's waiting."

I was so surprised I did not at once take it. Miss Starling set down her spoon to snatch and open the paper, for it was unsealed.

Iphigenia, reaching across my place at the table, read it next. "Ooh, lucky!"

She passed it to me. In a hastily elegant scrawl, it read:

> *Miss Oliver,*
> *I shall be at the Lost Bell all morning. If you will be*
> *so good as to attend me there, I hope to be the*
> *means of doing you a service—*
> *Yrs. v. sincerely, &c.,*
> *Diana Tassell*

"What do you think the service is?" Miss Starling asked, eyes bright.

"Maybe she has a husband for you," Iffy suggested. "Why not? She tried it with Phoebe Dymond."

"She must know of a child in town who wants to learn the guitar," I said tiredly, too out of sorts this morning to enjoy the game.

Smiles fading, my friends shrugged and turned back to their burnt breakfasts. A hollowness in my chest joined the hollowness in my stomach.

The Earl and Countess of Tassell were the Whig patrons of Lively St. Lemeston, here during Parliament's brief Easter recess to glad-hand, scatter largesse, and celebrate Holy Week. Even in their absence (which encompassed much of the year), their agent in the borough was kept very busy paying for funerals and finding apprenticeships for supporters of the local Whig party.

"Maybe her ladyship will have a collation laid out," Iphigenia said dreamily.

My spoon hovered over my bowl. Bad porridge was sure, a collation a faint hope. "Do you think she'll be in a generous mood? Last autumn's election was expensive *and* a failure."

Her eyes crinkled. "She's probably throwing good money after bad. People do."

I laughed. Iphigenia had always been an optimist, after her own cynical fashion. I was not, but if I was offered breakfast at the Lost Bell and was too full of oats to eat it, I would kick myself all week.

I pushed back my bowl—and poor Iphigenia pulled it towards herself. "It wouldn't do to keep her ladyship waiting," I said. "Please tell her footman I'll come straightaway."

Despite the early hour, Lively St. Lemeston's sidewalks and streets were thronged. Lent was the Sussex marbles season, and today's noon church bells would stop it short. Holding my skirts out of the mud—I wore every petticoat I owned against the cold, and washing-day was days away—I skirted chalked circles ringed with men and boys, competing with raucous good cheer and the occasional heated dispute.

Meanwhile, the local women skipped rope, a whole group on one long line swung by two people. They chanted and sang and laughed, cheeks rosy and eyes bright in the damp morning.

Lord Tassell and some of the other borough patrons joined in the marbles, heedless of muddy knees. But no ladies of equal rank joined the skipping, as they had when I was a girl. Lydia Cahill merely watched her husband's game, arms swallowed by her enormous muff; she would not even blow on his taw for luck until she had demurred for long moments, blushing. It seemed that spring grew chillier and the town's ladies more decorous with each year that went by.

I glanced down to be sure I was not lifting my petticoats too far out of the mud, and showing too much ankle.

At last I reached the Lost Bell. With so many people out-of-doors I had expected to find the coaching inn empty, but petitioners of every age and sex loitered in the corridor outside the Countess of Tassell's private parlor—some bored, some eager, and some desperate.

I hoped I was not one of the latter.

Yes, I was undeniably shabby-genteel in my faded pelisse and yellowing gloves. Yes, the soles of my boots were cracking. Yes, guitar pupils were in short supply. But I had paid my rent on Lady Day.

Barely, a scrupulous voice inside me amended. If I lost two pupils more, I might not manage it at Midsummer. And the boardinghouse mistress accepted nothing but cash in hand.

I pushed the thought away and stood straighter, hoping no one heard my stomach rumble at the smell of food wafting from the taproom.

At last a woman with ink-stained fingers asked me my business with Lady Tassell. I gave her the note I had received, summoning me. I could not help evaluating her as she checked the note against her memorandum book and ushered me into the august presence: unruly hair, but blonde; not English, but her accent was refined—Scottish at the worst; not beautiful, but her features pale and delicate; not young, but likely no older than my own thirty-four. I would have thought her a nobody if I passed her on the street. What had recommended her for her good position, and guaranteed her hearty meals and new clothes?

Quickly averting my gaze from the groaning sideboard, I sank into the deep curtsy due a countess.

Clinging to gentility by your fingernails! the voice said, scornful now. At boarding school, we had been led to imagine adorning ballrooms with our accomplishments, not trading upon them in rented offices. Alas, it developed that balancing a book on one's head was a profitable talent for a trained bear, not a woman.

Lady Tassell smiled, gesturing at the food. "Please, help yourself."

Magic words! Probably she had seen my eyes fly greedily to the spread, but shame could not overshadow my pleasure. I filled my plate with hot buttered toast, smoked herring, marmalade—

"The ham is particularly fine," she said.

I pretended I hadn't heard, cutting myself two generous slices of hard local cheese and hurrying to take the hard chair placed opposite Lady Tassell's writing table. Balancing my plate awkwardly on my knees, I bit into my toast with exquisite joy. When had I last eaten white bread?

Lady Tassell poured a cup of chocolate from a pot at her elbow. I did not dare hope. I did not dare look at the cup.

She slid it towards me.

My fingers shook with eagerness as I picked it up. I hoped she thought it nerves.

Ohhh… Bittersweet chocolate and rich cream caressed my tongue, whispering of lemon, cinnamon, and cloves. It lingered in my throat like Romeo in Juliet's bed. I inhaled the steam, despising Mrs. Humphrey's weak tea with all my heart.

"You have a lovely smile," Lady Tassell said.

I wiped it from my face at once. Did the countess know that was the secret hope of every plain woman—that some Midas touch in her smile would transform her narrow face, long nose, and limp, mousy hair? But no change of expression could render me lovely. When I was solemn my lips were too full for English fashion, and my smile bared horsey Oliver teeth. I was grateful enough for a new pupil without flattery.

But it would be unladylike to say so. "Thank you, my lady, you are very kind."

"You grew up in Portsmouth, didn't you? Are you fond of the sea?"

"Yes, my lady," I said, wondering at the question. "We came here when I was thirteen, after my mother died."

I rarely thought of the sea these days, but as a girl I had loved to walk along the harbor in good and ill weather, watching the men at work in the boats. My mother and I had shared a passion for combing the beach for shards of glass and pottery, worn smooth by the terrible endless friction of the waves. There was nothing so vast in Lively St. Lemeston. Low green hills bounded the horizon close on every side, and the River Arun barely deserved the title.

Yet I knew Lively St. Lemeston would wear me smooth and small enough in its time.

"Tassell Hall is only six or seven miles from the coast, but it's too far to smell the sea," Lady Tassell remarked. "At our lodge in Rye Bay, you can see the cliffs from the front windows."

I made a polite noise and took another sip of chocolate.

"One of my Rye Bay neighbors wants a governess for his little girl. I could think of no one else qualified for the role, who might be brave enough to travel so far from home. You have always struck me as a self-reliant young woman."

This was flattery, too—more dangerous than the first. If Lady Tassell truly thought me pretty, she would never recommend me for a governess. My friend Iphigenia, more scholarly and accomplished, had been refused half a dozen such posts over the years, precisely for her incandescent beauty.

But self-reliant? I could almost believe that of myself. I crunched my toast smugly between my big Oliver teeth.

I should have been wary. I should have known better than to think a little independence of spirit could arm me against all the danger of the wide world. But I was seduced by salt and sugar, chocolate and white flour.

"The pay is twenty-five guineas per annum, with room and board. I am told the child is obedient enough, though she's struck me as a little peculiar." The countess chuckled. "But what child isn't peculiar?"

I smiled back, mentally turning over that *room and board*. A governess wasn't family, but she was not a servant, either. Surely the food would be good, and the bed soft. A salary to be received on quarter-days, instead of rent to pay. "Is her mother dead?"

A shadow passed over Lady Tassell's face. "No, but very ill. She does not much leave her room."

My heart went out to that obedient, peculiar little girl. An image formed in my mind: a solemn, dark-eyed child, perhaps a little resentful of her lot, inclined to throw stones at birds and make up secret languages. "How old is she?"

"Five."

"Young for a governess, surely."

Her eyes searched my face. She tapped her pen against the desk, then set it down decisively. "Allow me to be blunt. Lady Palethorp is foreign. Sir Kit wishes his daughter to have a good genteel English education." She screwed up her mouth. "If you will forgive me for offering you a very awkward piece of advice, it might be better not to speak of your mother to him."

My cheeks heated. No one in Lively St. Lemeston had ever met my mother. Few of them troubled to remember anything about her. But of course Lady Tassell was the exception.

"These John Bull country squires can be small-minded," she said ruefully. "The Olivers' unimpeachable respectability and your good schooling should satisfy him."

In all honesty, I was unlikely to have discussed my mother in any case. I wasn't ashamed of her. On the contrary, I hated to expose her to slights. She had borne enough of those, alive—from the unimpeachable Olivers, no less. I knew better than Lady Tassell ever could, about the small-mindedness of John Bull squires.

I could almost smell the sea. I *could* smell a generous breakfast.

And that little half-English girl needed someone to take care of her. "I'll go."

"I'm glad to hear it." But to my surprise, Lady Tassell did not look entirely glad. She fussed with her pen again, then leaned in. "I hope you will write me and tell me of your progress. Please believe I mean to stand a friend to you, Miss Oliver."

I drew back—not physically, but in my mind. I felt my grandmother's fingers dig into my shoulder, felt her hot breath in my ear: *They'll say they're your friends. Don't believe them! They lie, they lie…*

I could never hear the word *friend* without remembering. Perhaps that was why I had so few. "Thank you, my lady. I am sensible of the honor you do me."

"Then you'll write?"

I nodded reluctantly, already itching to leave—to tell Iphigenia about the position, and be reassured by her admiring exclamations.

I felt a pang. Iffy and I weren't as close as we had been at school, but I would miss her.

The countess produced a little tin box, and held it out with a smile. I made myself take it, reading the neat motto on its lid: "*A Gift* FROM A *Friend.*" It had been painted, no doubt, by some other not-yet-desperate lady trying to wring a living from her accomplishments.

I twisted open the lid to find a hot cross bun inside. The sweet Easter rolls were lucky, people said; keeping one by the hearth protected a house from fire. Every Good Friday I considered saving one—and every year some faint scruple prevented me.

I turned the tin until the cross was only an enigmatic letter X. "What a kind thought, my lady. Happy Easter."

"Happy Easter, dear. Please don't forget to write."

Buy the book at books2read.com/WifeInTheAttic